LUISA VALENZUELA

(with Argentines)

▬

TRANSLATED FROM THE SPANISH
BY TOBY TALBOT

SIMON & SCHUSTER

New York   London   Toronto   Sydney   Tokyo   Singapore

SIMON & SCHUSTER
Simon & Schuster Building
Rockefeller Center
1230 Avenue of the Americas
New York, New York 10020

Copyright © 1990 by Luisa Valenzuela
English translation copyright © 1992 by Simon & Schuster Inc.
All rights reserved
including the right of reproduction
in whole or in part in any form.
Originally published in Spanish by Ediciones Del Norte as
Novela Negra Con Argentinos.

SIMON & SCHUSTER and colophon are registered trademarks
of Simon & Schuster Inc.
Designed by Pei Loi Koay
Manufactured in the United States of America

1 3 5 7 9 10 8 6 4 2

Library of Congress Cataloging-in-Publication Data
Valenzuela, Luisa, date
[Novela negra con argentinos. English]
Black novel with Argentines / Luisa Valenzuela : translated from
the Spanish by Toby Talbot.
p.   cm.
Translation of: Novela negra con argentinos.
I. Title.
PQ7798.32.A48N613   1992
863—dc20   92-9283
CIP

ISBN: 0-671-68764-6

*This novel, which was five years in the making, was launched by a grant
from the Guggenheim Foundation, for which I am profoundly grateful.*

L. V.

To Bolek Greczynski

PART

The man—thirty-fiveish, dark beard—comes out of an apartment, shuts the door carefully, checks that it can't be opened from the outside. The door, of solid oak, has a triple lock; the latch doesn't give. Over the bronze peephole it says 10H.

The action takes place on a Saturday toward dawn, on Manhattan's Upper West Side.

There is no audience.

The man, Agustín Palant—Argentine, a writer—has just killed a woman. In so-called reality, not in the slippery, ambiguous realm of fiction.

A woman lies dead inside the apartment, killed for no reason, in an unintentional act, perhaps concluding the melancholy act begun that autumn afternoon when the man entered a gun shop and bought a revolver. Just a .22.

He had a motive for going to Little Italy to buy the gun, but none whatsoever for raising it to the woman's temple and pulling the trigger.

These notions, perceptions, keep spinning through his mind as he furtively descends the stairs. He knows not to bring the elevator up to the floor of the crime, knows or intuits that he must leave no trail. He is also aware of the danger of running into someone; he must allow himself a few minutes to conceal his terror: an impossible task. At three A.M. on a rainy night like this he bumps into no one, no one's on the stairway of so respectable a building. Respectable as the woman in 10H, or so believes a murderer who with infinite caution creeps down the stairs.

This phrase forms in his mind word by word: "a murderer who with infinite caution."

Murderer? No, not him.

It can't be him. It could be a character in some trashy novel, or a ham actor totally alien to him. He feels an urge to vomit. He leans over, sees the stairway looming at his feet, feels about to plunge downward to the very core of the earth, to the innermost bowels of underground sewers, manages to contain his nausea and to straighten up. He staggers to the next floor. At which point there is no choice but to take the elevator and risk being seen. It would be worse to leave a trail of vomit: he might be tracked through his stomach contents, the traces of his bile, his gastric juices, all the repugnant intimacies of his body pointing at him like an accusatory finger. Fingers. Like those that once appeared in the garbage dump behind the general headquarters, in another country, another life, another life story—memories to be stifled.

In the elevator he collects himself, smooths his thick beard. Adjusts his tie, that *porteño*—that typical Buenos Aires—defense against an overwhelming city, the act of strangling oneself slightly in the daily service of one's sentence.

When the door opens automatically, he forces himself to place one foot after the other in order to leave the small elevator and face a potential captor. He moves forward as steadily as he can, trying to avoid attention at an hour when everybody ought to be sleeping, though not as soundly as the woman in 10H—no, not as deeply as the one up there, abandoned to her fate in the pitiless night.

Agustín Palant. Once outside the building he felt almost safe, but barely had time to take a deep breath. A voice practically on top of him shouted, "Hey, man! Why don'tcha look where ya goin'? Jus' 'cause I'm black, ya gonna step all ovuh me?"

"No sir, not me. I just need a breath, some fresh air."

"I have a right to breathe too, motherfucker. You're takin' my air, man."

As the drunk staggered away down West End Avenue shouting obscenities, Agustín felt his legs give way beneath him. He leaned against a wall, thinking that maybe it would be better to just give himself up. To surrender little by little, member by member, beginning with those legs that refused to remain accomplices of a body that had eliminated another body with such awesome, unexpected ease.

A beautiful woman's body, that other one. A young actress playing her final role, stretched out on the carpet of her own bedroom with a hole in her temple, possibly drained of blood by now. He had not been able to lower his eyes to look at her. Merely registered the sound of the unexpected shot, which still echoed inside his head. One more explosion in an explosive city, an almost point-blank shot, for a .22 can't be expected to kill at a distance. Expected to kill? And why? Especially this woman who had done him no harm, who was apparently ready to do him all the good in the world.

He had killed a stranger for no reason, without the slightest motive. Inconceivable. It was even laughable, and he did just that—he began to laugh involuntarily. Crazy laughter welled up without control, slowly at first, spreading out like a flash fire that races through the forest and devours trees, reducing everything to cinders. Sooty guffaws blackening and weakening him, his legs giving way under his body, and the chill of the night piercing his lungs.

Desperation brought tears to his eyes. Desperation, and the laughter, and the pain he felt for the poor woman he had just killed. Pain for himself, too, for with that pointless death he in turn was dying a little. Or might die altogether. In the electric chair.

He crouched against a wall, completely spent. Out of the corner of his eye he saw a cop looking at him unbenevolently. He'd end up arrested for loitering—what a shitty way to get caught. No, that wouldn't do. He decided to protect himself as much as he could, though it might be too late for that. His legs must respond, dammit. Tighten up, get him on his feet. He took a few hesitant steps, tottering as though they were his very first. He had to resist, above all, the temptation to catch a cab; had to get away without drawing attention; leave no traces or witnesses behind.

He'd need to disappear into the anonymity of crowds, but at this hour only a few late-nighters were about, and a cop who kept his eyes glued on him. Just walk to the subway station without turning around, feeling the cop's eyes riveted on the nape of his neck, like in a sleazy novel, feeling himself inside one of those novels he would have liked to write but not this way, not with the body, as Roberta would say. Force himself to reach the subway entrance somewhat stiffly, promising himself a taxi farther on, when there'd be no need for concealment. When he'd feel safer, because he was taking the No. 1 train, which wasn't his line—that indecipherable web of the New York subway system in which he didn't care to get trapped.

Shit, Agustín Palant said to himself, imagine coming to this city for refuge and winding up so true to the trashy local reading matter, so very untrue to his only concern, his writing.

He'd never be able to get back to writing again. At least not until he understood why he had put the gun to a head and pulled the trigger. To that particular head. She was, had been, an actress and her name was Edwina. He remembered the name well, had repeated it many times in the previous hours: in the theater, on the way to her place, even inside the apartment and perhaps at the very instant he had drawn the gun. E-dwi-na, pronounced like that, the syllables elongated slightly, as everyone pronounced it who approached, like him, to congratulate her after the performance. To congratulate her and to partake of the soup she had prepared in the course of the play. But that's another story—though the soup in fact was to blame for what subsequently ensued, because it provided the break that gave them both time to chat. He must have appeared interesting to her, with his black beard and his intelligent, slightly stiff manner. They had agreed to have a drink together one of these nights. And Agustín, as he was leaving the warehouse that had been converted into a theater, decided—without pausing to think of Roberta, who'd be waiting for him—that this night would be the night, this very dire, ill-omened night.

In her corner of the Village, like a boxer warming up in the opposite corner of the ring, Roberta is dancing her thoughts, a glass of slivovitz in her hand. The fight might seem to be against all the internal scabs that tend to block the noble flow of secret material, were it not for sporadic flashes of Agustín—Agustín's name, the anticipation of an embrace, of a word—which interfere and waylay her. A kind of yearning that springs from much farther away and can at this point turn into shadow.

Tonight her primordial sensation is of galloping. Galloping energy. That's what she likes best. If she were writing, she would write the word "energy" with a capital *E,* but she is dancing—though actually writing in a much more physical form: with her body. It is writing without leaving marks, for one reader, herself. That is how she loves herself most. Neither very crafty nor very subtle, nor even elegant (though she has known such moments), she can truly love herself only when riding energy as though it were a colt. Or rather, a broomstick. Witch that you are, she says to herself.

Her concern over dear Agustín pops up intermittently but is exorcisable, today. How she'd like to grab him by his hair and demand, Love me, dammit! She'd enjoy some violent reaction on his part—a crushing embrace, a rejection, anything that would relate him to her, but not that amorphous evasiveness of his, like an unwilled loving, or the other way around.

Tonight she'd like to distance herself from Agustín, from the memory of him, from the need of him, or rather, from the need to have him change and respond fully to her need. Tonight Roberta is determined to get back to work on her new novel. No sooner had she met Agustín a few months back than she lost the thread of the story, and now that she's managing to recapture it, her characters are no longer tractable. They have rebelled, and refuse to conform to the outline; they are getting out of hand. So much the better. Roberta the author is painfully coming back to herself. In this novel she'd set out to be someone else, methodical and structured—not because of Agustín Palant's influence, as might be assumed, but as a premonition of Agustín, who would intrude in her life and mess up the plot.

They'd met at one of those writers' conferences that flourish in New York. Latin American writers, to top it off. Agustín Palant had just arrived here on a major grant and Roberta liked his looks. Glances flew back and forth; they recognized each other at a distance: colleagues, compatriots, those affinities of the spirit coupled with other, more secret attractions. At the closing reception of the conference he approached her, glass in hand.

"Roberta Aguilar—is that a pen name? I've read some of your things."

"So have I. I mean, not my things, yours. Those so-called novels—I was taken by them. You have a real gift for detail, but a kind of sinister gift, more agonizing than Proustian. Forgive me. That's no way to talk at a gringo gathering."

"In any case, I intend to write differently now. I'd like to put in more mud, more blood, or something. That sounds phony, corny. Now it's your turn to forgive me."

"Deep down in our little souls we'll always be pusillanimous *porteños*, Buenos Aires guys always apologizing for the bit of sincerity we dare to express."

"And how! Facing the terror of million-eyed skyscrapers watching us in the neon night, we remain *porteños*. But I won't let that deter me from telling you that I read your stories with pleasure, though at times I found them somewhat reckless, a headlong plunge into the void."

"You, on the other hand, have turned out to be quite rational when you pen up the pick. I mean, when you pick up the pen."

"No. You meant the first and said it. Bravo. I know you from your writing and I like what I know, I feel we're complementary."

"Don't scare me. Sounds casebook, doesn't it? Impulsive girl and rational, well-balanced boy."

"Not exactly. In what little of yours I've read I thought I detected some weird reasoning that balanced impulse. As for me, I try to find what's illogical in the logical."

"One does what one can."

"And whatever else, to boot."

"If you say so."

From lip to kip, nary a slip. Roberta had been living in New York for five years when they met. Agustín was thinking he would spend his grant year prowling the city and environs, writing a novel and using up his funds. But the novel wasn't progressing, as he admitted to Roberta when their meetings became more intimate. The novel wasn't progressing, and on certain occasions like this one intimacy wasn't progressing too well either. Perhaps writing and intimacy were in some secret way connected, Roberta thought then, without daring to say so.

"Don't worry," she reassured him instead. "Don't focus specifically on the novel, write with the body. It's the only thing that can provide a glimmer of truth."

"I don't know what you mean by that."

"Well, I don't know either, but I feel it. Write with the body, I tell you. The secret is *res, non verba*. Restore, renew, re-create. See what I mean? Words lead you by the nose. They practically pull you along, often make you stumble. 'Fallen woman' I might be called by one of those philistines so abundant *chez nous*. Sure. We're all whores of language. We work for it, feed it, humble ourselves on its account; we brag about it—and in the end, what? Language demands more. It will always be asking us to give more, to delve deeper. Like in our crowded buses: one step back, please, which means a step farther in, farther into that fathomless depth from which it becomes increasingly hard to emerge and then plunge in again. That's why I say to write with the body, because the poor little head can't make it on its own to the bottomless bottom—in spite of any analogy, metaphor, association, or allegory your feverish brain may be concocting at this moment."

Roberta, ever canny at motivating the other. Quick on the draw with lip service, only to be plunged then into an anxiety that can be dispelled only at a gallop. Not until then does she feel mistress of herself, in the arms of a man or in the arms of what she calls the energy, which in the best of times impels her to write, and in the worst (now) prompts her to ask herself where in the world Agustín could be, why he has not shown up.

3

With agonizing effort Agustín Palant finally attained his purpose: he went underground. That is, he descended the subway stairs, bought a token, passed through the turnstile, stood straight on his feet, and tried to breathe with near-human regularity, no longer like an animal at bay. All he needed now was for the train to take him out of that horror zone. Out of himself. If that were possible.

At this late hour the wait could be endless. He knew how infrequently trains ran at night, knew of the delusion and emptiness of the night, the ominous night to which there was now added a much more anguishing threat: the loss of self-recognition, ensnared forever in the trap of a death. A woman's death. Edwina's. Edwina who? as his mother would have asked long ago. Never give first names without corresponding surname, and middle name if possible; never give only the first name—it's coarse, vulgar. Given names, aliases, surnames, nicknames, pet names—whose nickname is it, whose alias? What was her name? *What was her name?* the interrogator screamed, or would scream if Agustín Palant was ever interrogated.

Edwina who? A common name, ordinary—Brown, Jones, Smith. Agustín reached into the pocket of his raincoat, pulled out the photocopied page—the theater program—and read: Edwina Irving. That was it. Instantly he realized what he was holding in his hand, crumpled it into a ball, and tossed it far away as if he were pulling a tick off his body. His heart began to thump. He looked around in terror and saw that no one was watching him, no one suspected. Only three people were on the platform, minding their own business. A drunk dozing in his urine and a couple kissing: two men with identical mustaches, kissing as though this were their last chance. He edged over to the discarded ball of paper that had been the program and picked it up, intending to set it on fire, but held himself back to avoid drawing attention from those seemingly self-absorbed bystanders. He began tearing it casually into shreds, as though filling in that timeless waiting time, while he sauntered over to the trash bin and scattered the confetti among the empty cans, greasy containers, tattered newspapers, the paper cups and vomit and other vile human waste in this utterly visceral city, capital of filth.

That's what he remembered thinking: the garbage and the city and the vomit—precisely that when he decided to head for the zone, to explore unknown territories. Don't dream of going there, he was told a few days after arriving in New York. The Lower East Side is as dangerous as Harlem at the other end of the city, crawling with pushers. Better keep away, never go east of First—that's the borderline. But if one doesn't cross borders, can one ever get to the other side? Roberta had probably popped that question into his head; it was her off-the-cuff kind of remark, jabbed into the listener like a banderilla. Hitting Avenue C, for example, crossing the alphabet at some point, she'd most likely suggested it, though it was easy to lay the blame on her now. Penetrate the alphabet with the body, Roberta might well have said during an innocuous stroll. In fact, he *had* penetrated it. Alone. Or not entirely. A few blocks earlier, on the safe side of the border but close to the edge, he'd entered the gun shop alone and had emerged accompanied by a gun.

If he was to accept that offer of an isolated house in the Adirondacks—the ideal place, he was assured, to get down to writing his novel—he'd need what little feeling of security a gun could provide. Just to put up a show, to scare off a would-be robber, if any should dream of mugging a mere writer forsaken even by his muse.

All so neat, meticulously planned. Someone had once dropped a remark about a certain gun shop where all sorts of weapons could be purchased, no questions asked. And he'd gone precisely to that place, to that narrow, foul-smelling alley behind the beautiful, massive wedding-cake structure that *in illo tempore* had been police headquarters, of all things.

I need something of small caliber, simple, just to give me a sense of security, he told them at the gun shop. They looked at him contemptuously, and even more so when he asked to have the bullets wrapped separately. It's not a good idea to go around this town with an unloaded gun, he remembered being nudged. At the counter they showed him how to crack the cylinder and insert the bullets, and told him it was all set, and slipped the revolver into his jacket pocket and warned him, he believes, When you carry a weapon, you gotta be alert. Imagine.

They're all nuts, Agustín had said to himself coming out of the shop, but humiliation gradually gave way to a sense of power as he drew closer to the border and crossed it without thinking. He walked towards Tompkins Square, and it was getting dark.

With the security of a gun in his pocket, with the absurdity of carrying a loaded weapon for the first time in his life, Agustín penetrated deeper into the grim disaster area. On this side or the other, he thought, the filth is the same, always the same piles of black plastic bags full of refuse, but in my country when the military junta was in power the bags might contain the remains of . . . Well, better think of something else, put on a smile of assurance, act alert without showing alarm, walk with confidence amid those voices offering inhalable, absorbable, injectable drugs, offering him women, men, teenagers, children, and telling him credit cards accepted, anything, as he made his way through the human misery, pretending not to hear, because that's the form of communication in these strata, some talking or yelling into the air with terrible lunatic cries, hawking the lures and poetic names of heroin that sound like tropical paradises to the ears of the desperate who've dragged themselves from afar in response to the call of those who shout but never look anyone in the eye, those who pretend never to be the sellers of what they sell as their customers pretend never to be the buyers of what they buy. Thus Agustín slips—slipped—through that deranged region feeling himself untouched.

He crossed creepy Tompkins Square diagonally, or so it seemed, letting himself be drawn along by shadows. He covered blocks he would previously have shunned even in broad daylight, felt the courage flowing from the loaded gun in his jacket pocket, hidden under his raincoat but so very conspicuous in his smile. He'd never be capable of using it, but meanwhile the feeling of security impelled him on.

And gradually he recognized and to some extent accepted the other face—or rather, the dark, delinquent asshole—of this ever elusive, ever changing city.

Roberta would be proud of him, but he wouldn't tell Roberta. He didn't want to hand her this victory. Put your body where your words are, she had demanded of him in one way or another, more in connection with their relationship than with writing. He wasn't planning to write about these areas of detritus where the city became deadly, much truer to itself than in Park Avenue's neat geometry, for example. Agustín loved to walk along Park without Roberta, because Roberta felt her heart constrict there in a way she couldn't describe to Agustín but that she associated with the physically unattainable: the unbounded, the frigid, the beautiful, the missing.

Roberta's name flickers in his memory as he waits for the lights to come into view at the end of the tunnel. Now he's surprised that she never even crossed his mind during his long stroll beyond the border, when he finally accepted one of the countless offers along the way. Maybe he accepted it because it was free, maybe because the guy offering it was not one of the pushy or sneaky ones. The guy looked straight at him, sized him up, came right over and handed it to him. An innocuous theater ticket. An offer you can't refuse, the fellow said, 'cause it's a gift and 'cause it's an excellent play. And then he added, I myself can't go, but you won't regret it; the group is great and will be well known real soon. But meanwhile it's playing underground, open to chance, for chance plays a leading role in this work in progress.

Space and time worked in his favor, if that could be said in the light of subsequent events. The theater was a few blocks from the corner where he'd met the stranger, and the stranger escorted him to the door. The houselights were dimming as Agustín entered. A spotlight came up on a secondary but essential character who was preparing a soup. Making soup—who could have imagined, on a stage so far from reality, so far from Broadway? The scene was completely unrelated to the cook, but was punctuated by her snapping the vegetables with her hands or chopping them on a board. On the stove was a steaming caldron into which she threw salt and noodles. She chopped the vegetables, while a man kept crossing back and forth, lugging an enormous old-fashioned typewriter. Every now and then he'd climb on top of it to deliver a tirade as various characters appeared and reappeared, transformed. Agustín paid scant attention to them. His eyes were on the woman with the soup— probably beautiful, perhaps evoking in him old memories of household aromas—and after the final applause he accepted the invitation extended to the audience to come up to the stage at the center of the warehouse and share the hearty soup.

There, between spoonfuls, actress and bearded playgoer spoke little, but gazed at one another and exchanged intentions to meet again.

"I'll be back one of these nights and we can get together for a drink," said Agustín. She nodded happily.

He was not going to come back. He was going to hang around outside the theater since he did not know his precise whereabouts. He was going to wait for her, not wanting to acknowledge that he was waiting, until he saw her emerge by herself through a small side door and he followed her for a couple of blocks working up the courage to approach her. We're going the same way, he finally managed to say, and she replied, I don't think so. I live far from here. All right, he told her, then we're going the same way because I want to accompany you. I'll go wherever you're going, I don't even know where I am, and you'll have to get me out of this godforsaken place, this sinister maze, but don't be afraid, I'll protect you.

Arrogant like all men, she may or may not have thought, not knowing the guy, as she led him around corners and through long alarming blocks to the subway. As they descended the steps, she said, When I walk through places like this, I always take out my keys and grip them in my hand in a hard fist. Like this. In case of an attack. But now you're here to protect me, right?

Wrong.

That he now knows, in this other subway station, waiting for a train that never comes, and anyway wouldn't take him to his destination. He begins walking toward the end of the long platform, but immediately turns back to the more brightly lit protected area, where the drunk has fallen asleep in his private puddle. The urine must have felt warm when it welled out of the drunk as from a friendly spring, but now it is just another one of the infinite frozen piss puddles in this urinal city bristling with piss crystals—thorns Agustín feels he could roll around on, merging the cold and his own sweat. Sweating endlessly, profusely, revoltingly, imcomprehensibly—like everything else tonight—his pores reacting but not he, he without an answer, with only questions, beaded like the drops of perspiration, and the why—why did I do it?—mingling with practical considerations: What may I have left behind in that apartment? What telltale evidence, what part of me and not just my soul, may have remained there to give me away?

Another figure appears on the platform and starts walking slowly toward Agustín. Agustín stiffens, wants to run away, is halted by the wall, pretends to be smoothing his beard but is actually covering up a look of horror. He would have liked to alter his face, be somebody else. Gotta light? the guy asks or demands, almost upon him now. No, no, Agustín replies, shaking his head, burying his hand in his raincoat pocket in a fruitless search. No, no, his hand then opens the raincoat and reaches into the jacket pocket, where it finds the other cold, metallic fire.

He was fully dressed when it happened. Fully dressed. He had taken off only his raincoat, which he'd had the presence of mind to grab on his way out. They had already reached the bedroom, and he was about to remove his jacket, but instead he put his hand into his right pocket, felt the revolver which he'd forgotten about, took it out, and then.

Everything that had taken place previously with Edwina had been a sweet game of recognition, with voices first and then with hands, with long silences in front of the fireplace and that wondrous perception of the fingertips, and suddenly without saying a word she'd stood up and headed for the bedroom. He too stood up, to follow her, vaguely regretting having to abandon his cozy nook.

It was her open smile when she turned around in the middle of the bedroom that invited Agustín to come to her. And as he was about to take her in his arms, he reached into his jacket pocket and did what he did without ever imagining it, only to remain transfixed by a dull explosion and an act that seemed to belong to someone else.

At last the train arrives. Agustín rushes to a car other than the one the rest of the people on the platform are entering. For a while at least, he feels that he has escaped outside threat. But not the other threat. His car is empty except for a Chinese family, a mother and three children all sound asleep, the father grimly determined to remain awake. Obviously the man has carefully read the overhead signs: DON'T FALL ASLEEP, DON'T INVITE ROBBERY. Agustín generally heeded these and other municipal warnings. Now he couldn't care less. Watch out, he'd been warned before leaving Buenos Aires. Don't take risks, don't go out at night, don't go around alone after six P.M., don't dream of going into Central Park even in broad daylight. New York is the most dangerous city. Beware. He'd been petrified by the kindly souls of Barrio Norte who never set foot outside the neighborhood. And he had made provisions to protect himself against aggression, never dreaming he'd need protection against himself as aggressor. With the tragic result of two victims: the dead woman and himself, who through an inconceivable act had become utterly incapable of self-recognition.

It was like passing your hands over your arms, your shoulders, chest, and being unable to find yourself, no longer knowing who you are or what it's all about. And now when he achieves a glimmer of something resembling lucidity, when the memory and the horror are not overwhelming, all he can do is doubt his soundness of mind. A fit of madness would be the most sensible explanation of his act, and being sensible, he dismisses it. Too simple. I went crazy, returned to normal, nothing has happened here. No. He's going to have to talk to Roberta, ask her what she thinks might have happened, consult Roberta after having confessed everything to her. Roberta? Why, only now, is he thinking of turning to her, his one friend in this remorseless city? Could it be that he doesn't love her? Or that precisely because he does, it hadn't occurred to him to involve her? Could it be that he has killed because he loves her, to avoid betraying her?

As though the relationship with Roberta were that close, as though they were tightly bound to each other, not merely together occasionally, when he can't take it anymore and succumbs, abandons his papers, temporarily gives up his attempts to write and runs to Roberta who is into her own novel and has no pity for him. Roberta demands more and perhaps has it in mind to use him as a character. Sometimes he feels squeezed into a pulp and pressed between the covers of one of Roberta's books, as if he were the one to engender all writing, as if she hadn't written and published long before knowing him, as if literature were instigated by him, rather than created by him, with his own pen. With his own hand.

It would seem that nothing gets created by his hand, only killed: if one is unable to give life, one kills. Kills? That cannot have happened to me. No, not me. It wasn't me, he felt when he saw that stranger, Edwina, falling. And he remained stunned, gun in hand, like a double of himself. It wasn't me who pulled the trigger and shot and killed someone. Absolutely not.

Precisely because of that, more myself than ever—more himself than ever because of the simple fact of viewing himself from the outside.

The revolver. Luckily he'd returned it to his pocket, hadn't left it behind to give him away.

He knows he cannot escape from guilt even if he manages to escape justice. Nor can he escape from Roberta, his only link to reality.

Now, through the black tunnels, at full screeching speed, shaken and tossed about by the express train blurring the stations, he tries to think clearly. To look around in the car, to recover.

He pays no attention to the stops. He is being left to himself, and he notices a teenager at the opposite end of the car, printing his name in elaborate calligraphy with a felt-tip marker. Curtis, Curtis, Curtis, on every writable surface, on the subway map, on ads, on the walls, the windows, and door exactly where someone more sophisticated than Curtis has edited one of the bilingual warning signs: *No se apoye contra la puerta*/Do not lean against the door, to read: *No apoye la contra*/Do not support the contras. Curtis, without reading or understanding anything, writes over it, stamping his brand with graphomanic zeal.

Agustín closes his eyes to shut out the alien name inexorably covering all available space, the mobile world. The name is now inscribed even upon the metal seats; soon he, the only fellow traveler, will be written upon. I too have my place, have my inscription, he repeats to himself, and finds this hard to believe. What is my place?

the one going from the barrel of a gun to a woman's temple
the brief trajectory of a bullet shot almost point-blank
the duration of a shot.

Maybe his jacket was inscribed in blood in the space/time of the disaster. Luckily not his face—he'd seen himself in the elevator mirror. Not his face but maybe his jacket, his shirt. He buttons his raincoat up to the collar, trying to blot himself out.

I was not here, he would write if that were logical, if he were not giving himself away by a denial of that magnitude. Agustín was not here. But of course Agustín is where he claims not to be. And where he believes himself to be what is happening?

Saturday afternoon and Roberta is no longer galloping any energy at all. Now she just wants to finish her novel tamely, at a slow trot, and feels that the novel has abandoned her. Inspiration, the muse, or whatever it was is no longer with her. Nor is Agustín around to encourage her, even though he's the one who usually demands encouragement, which also worries her: Agustín makes demands and goes off, throws a stone and acts innocent.

Writing seems to have lost its inner life. What had been sheer flight and stimulation is now leaden and dragging Roberta down. Best to leave off writing for the time being, get out and roam those damned streets. Not be caught in the double trap of waiting, waiting for both Agustín and the novel. Get out and see someone, whoever, the person closest at hand.

Ava Taurel, as she calls herself, asks the men who frequent her:
Soft bondage? Hard bondage?
Leather? Chains?
Do you favor wearing women's undies? Spike heels?
Do you fancy extreme pain or slight pain? Whips? Suffocation?
Ava explains all this to Roberta, who has dropped in for a visit. Roberta listens, detached. Roberta transformed into an ear. And Ava Taurel, the mouth, goes on: I seek the human spirit beyond pain; I want to find out how much the body can take, and then go just a bit beyond, to push that limit. I'm interested

in limits. They tell me, That's it, and I go that far, with an additional twist of the tourniquet to see what happens.

Limits and abysses, whatever. Some time before, Roberta had been discussing this question with Agustín, but those were limits of a different kind, not of physical pain but of the terrifying, unattainable possibility of mutual understanding. (When we're together, I feel a wall that I want to push against. You have a terribly tractable wall inside you, which is your strongest attraction. I want to see you from the other side of that wall even if it hurts.) On the other hand, physical pain sounds so utterly banal to Roberta, so bereft of imagination despite the mouth's efforts to convince her otherwise.

There had been an opening dialogue, and at the outset the ear-to-be (already beginning to turn into one) came to identify with the mouth. This identification broke down after the fourth or fifth remark but left something pending between them. It was at a typical book party that the mouth-to-be launched into the exercise of her craft as such, breaking the ice by asking Roberta about her love life. We've met several times now, said Ava Taurel to Roberta, and all I know about you is that you're a writer. Tell me more.

At first Roberta failed to understand that this tell me, this apparent demand to know and to hear, was simply an opening wedge. Roberta, not yet the ear, replied, My love life? Mixed up. She was on the verge of mentioning Agustín Palant, when the other woman picked up the thread again and added, So's mine. Men look at the great big blonde that I am and think I'm a Valkyrie—they're afraid of me.

How could Roberta avoid identification? Though she was neither big nor blond but quite the contrary, her eardrum vibrated, malleus struck incus, stapes resonated, and she became the ear itself, in expectation of words that would sketch her own portrait.

But the mouth, devoted to her trade, aroused no further sympathetic vibrations. She aroused the unconfessable.

I have two lovers and a slave, the mouth would relate. Divide and conquer, the mouth would say. A what? the ear would ask, barely showing a spark of repressed surprise. A slave, a slave of the kind one kicks and humiliates, provokes and disarms, a slave. I could have more than one, but to be a real slave a man must be worthy of it, must be of a certain stature, level with the soles of my feet, worshiping them. On Sundays I work in a torture chamber—didn't you know?—where I'm called upon to bring all my knowledge into play as well as my psychological training, for there are tortures of all kinds, and they require technique but, above all, imagination, true creativity, which I have galore.

(And the ear becomes a light in her own brain that switches on the other distant torture scene into which her friends, brothers, compatriots, were unwillingly caught, without the slightest possibility of pleasure, only of pain.) The mouth tells of the pleasure. And don't think it's prostitution—nothing of the sort. We are dominatrices, responsible professionals; we provide a very positive social service. Imagine all those men loose in the world with no one to enact their fantasies for them. Our services are in demand by high-ranking executives. It's delicate work; men tired of always being boss want to be dominated, bossed around. (There are the torturers and the tortured, thought the ear; there are those with absolutely no desire to submit who are made to submit, who are dominated.) Tensions must be released, concludes the mouth.

Nipple clamps? Light? Heavy?

Genital torture? Light? Heavy?

(Cross out what does not apply.)

The two are now in the mouth's quarters, strewn with books, cassettes, records, folders, clothing on hangers or thrown over chairs. The ritual paraphernalia is nowhere in sight but evident in every object. The mouth had already informed her on the other occasion: I work in a place that has a stage for more or less public presentations, and separate cubicles where each dominatrix keeps her instruments and practices her craft. Also, I have my private practice.

The mouth had invited the ear to visit her workplace. It will give you ideas, you being a novelist, she had told her. The ear hadn't wanted to go that far—and she wasn't talking about city blocks—but in search of a certain form of truth she had gone to see the mouth in her den. And the mouth is wearing bright pink overalls, the color of a tongue, and struts about as though all of her were talking.

Much later on, the ear will return home asking herself why she has listened to all that, and even more, why she has glanced through those specialized magazines and agreed to leaf through Ava Taurel's secret correspondence. None of it is of any use for enriching her novel or attracting Agustín if Agustín doesn't show up. Though who knows? In any case, he might appreciate the fine irony of this story when she tells it to him, if she ever does. On the way home she buys the *New York Post* for the TV page. Her answering machine has no messages of any interest, and rather than bother to open the paper or turn on the TV, she's off to bed in her woolen socks.

At home, in his bed, Agustín just huddles up in his own cocoon, drenched. Maybe he could ask for help, but he knows there is no help for him. What he was looking for in the streets from the time he left the subway until he wound up in his apartment was something else. Punishment perhaps. He'd wandered for hours, thinks he had a few drinks in some scruffy bars, thinks he got rained on, but is uncertain whether his clothes are soaked with rain or with sweat. Not wanting to know, he pulls them off, and remains only with the guilt.

Two nights seem to have elapsed without his being aware of whether he's dreaming or actually experiencing anxiety, whether the horror stems from this side of wakefulness or the other. At times, half-consciously, he waits for a knock on the door and for someone to come and get him. Or for the door to be smashed in, as he was told happened in his country around the time he left it.

He remains plunged in the fitful semiwakefulness of fear.

Why did he dream of being tied down? Was it a dream? He was sprawled on the ground, hands and feet bound, arms askew and legs spread apart like a woman in labor—or as he imagined a woman in labor—feeling not about to give birth but to be quartered. The only thing missing were four horses to wrench out his extremities, though in this case it wasn't four horses and riders but one huge woman who dominated the scene. A terrifying woman, a primeval witch, and himself naked at first but then dressed in women's fishnet hose, a garter belt, and around his waist a maid's white apron ruffled in lace. The woman may have been Roberta but not altogether—it was another Roberta caressing his hairy chest with an expression not in the least caressing. That other Roberta ripped off his apron with revulsion. He just lay there in his black leather briefs, prick sticking out, and Roberta, who was no longer Roberta, her tits and huge enlarged nipples protruding, started to laugh, laugh, her belly quivering beneath the skimpy scarlet-studded heart that covered it. A flaming heart not where the heart actually is, and red spike-heeled boots piercing his heart—his actual heart, pounding desperately.

In fact, it's the telephone bell, which doesn't quite tear Agustín from that wakeful nightmare. In must be daytime, he thinks, someone must know or be after me—whereupon the woman in red boots reappears and once more he's staked to the floor, bound even tighter with chains, on the verge of being quartered, the woman no longer laughing but weeping, her scalding tears falling on his chest and below, at the very edge of the leather briefs where his engorged prick protrudes. Now without arms and legs, he has but one remaining member, the real one, the most protruberant, seared by the woman's tears. Not truly tears but wax from a candle the woman's hand draws ever closer, dripping the hot wax drop by drop on his prick, which doesn't lose its erection but quite to the contrary becomes more engorged, the edge of his leather briefs digging into him as he twists in desperation and pain beneath the chains. Now he is completely shackled, head imprisoned in a pillory, writhing, the woman kicking him with her spike heels, shouting, Say thank you, my mistress. Say it. Thank you, he barely mumbles, and another sharp kick pierces his lip. Thank you, my mistress.

The woman inserts one of her large nipples into his mouth. Suck, she commands, and the substance he suckles from that breast is like lava, and he suckles and suckles as the wax keeps flaying his prick. Now he is burning inside and out, until that

34

terrible spasm when the woman extinguishes the candle on his penis.

He is left gasping in that inferno. And the woman: Look, look, I got the imprint. Open your eyes, say Thank you, mistress. Say it, Thank you, mistress. The impression took, it came out perfect. Look.

And as his eyes open, the woman's face takes on the same gentle smile Edwina had moments before the disaster.

To escape the nightmare he jumped out of bed and crawled to the bathroom. Turned on both faucets and stuck himself on all fours under the shower, ice-cold to begin with and then scalding hot. His body, stiff at first, without any sensation of temperature, gradually relaxed under the warming water, enabling him to relieve himself right there in the tub. A foul stench arose from him and he lay as if dead but relieved, plunged in his own shit, his urine and semen, immersed in all that which the water now cleansed, reviving him. A feeling of thirst made him conscious of physical needs and he opened his mouth wide, face uptilted, to allow the shower water to cleanse his insides.

Still in flannel pajamas and her woolen socks, looking like a true homebody, Roberta dialed Agustín's number again. She had called an hour before and gotten no answer. Strange for him not to be at home so early in the morning. She began to worry, but not too much, knowing how evasive he could be. Maybe he was sound asleep when the phone rang. But she persisted, needing to ask him a key question: What do you do with a character who takes off on his own, goes and does what he wants, throwing your novel off kilter?

Agustín would realize that when one speaks of novels, one implies something else. He would understand. That is, he'd understand if she ever got to question him, but the phone went unanswered, apparently ringing in a void.

An inhabited void, as was proved minutes later when the phone rang at Roberta's and it was Agustín, a voice like Agustín's coming from hell, in turn questioning, desperately trying to trace a call.

"Was that you a little while ago? Did you call?"

Taken aback, Roberta abandoned her question and her concern of just a few moments earlier. She chose to be the pursued, not the pursuer.

"No. I didn't call. What's up?"

Agustín found it hard to return to the surface of things. He finally managed it:

"I don't know. I feel rotten. I'll call you back."

"What's wrong? You sound awful. I'll come over and give you a hand. Make some tea, give you a massage."

"No. Absolutely not."

Agustín remained with the receiver in his hand and a further question: Who could have called him if not Roberta? Who might be tracking him? The sound of the phone had wrested him from one nightmare only to confront him with another. One more threat from the outer world slithering in between his damp sheets.

There he would stay, dying of starvation amid his own excrement, like the subway drunk, like all the forsaken of the world.

Just then he heard a thud outside his front door and feared that someone must be trying to get in. He felt a flash of heat, the tensing of muscles, and then nothing, a slackening, a cooling down, a calmer breathing, as he realized that it was the newspaper boy dropping the paper outside his lair. So it was Sunday, and awaiting him a few steps away was the pregnant Sunday edition, which he'd never ever be able to face again because it would carry the news. The item would fill the tabloids, and never again could he touch that rough paper reeking of printer's ink, of irrevocable event.

Never would he summon the courage to face it, to read it through, though it might, despite the abominable style of police reporting, inform him about Edwina, provide a clue. What deity had he sacrificed her to, if indeed it was a sacrifice? Who had pressed the trigger for him? Who deep inside him, utterly alien to him, had issued the command? He might learn something about that youthful aborted life, as the story would phrase it, about the brilliant career he'd nipped in the bud. His own name—that he wouldn't see in the newspapers, and though it might one day crop up, never again would he see his own name. The person he thought he was until the moment of the shot had never existed.

The other man there in his bed would languish in bed till he died of despair and disease.

Edwina's face appeared before him, Edwina's gentle smile at the very moment when he'd taken the revolver from his pocket. When he should have taken out something else, when he could have responded to her smile with his entire body and not simply with a vicious finger pressing a trigger.

It was as if he'd had to freeze that smile forever and engrave it in death. Death. He used to doodle with his pen to escape it but had managed with the point of another instrument to summon it.

Death provoked by his own courting and beckoning of it. As if wanting to drain his every breath of life.

Huddled between his wretched damp sheets, he tries desperately to retrieve Roberta's image, like a talisman—not the smile of the dead woman but the live, mocking smile—to recall the crazy things Roberta says, her absurd theory of writing with the body. Is it possible that what one writes with the body will seek erasure via some other, murdered body? His body had produced a trashy novel, an awful episode, messy handwriting, splotches of blood, and now the page cannot—ever—be turned again.

Edwina's image can't be so easily banished. Unexpected reminders of her body erupt—a hand serving him a glass of white wine, that gentle swell peeking out when the neckline of her sweater slipped over her shoulder, the rear view of her hips as she headed toward the bedroom: those conventional props of desire, everything but desire itself, and Edwina's face, and that name with its surprising familiarity. The day before yesterday he'd been totally unaware of her existence, and this morning, today (but is there a today? A yesterday? What time could it be, was there an exact hour, or was he immersed in death as in a timeless well?), now, he was contaminated by her. Like a blood pact with a single stream of blood coursing through them both.

(And what if she wasn't dead after all? He had verified nothing, had dashed out like the great coward he was, a killer despite himself, leaving her alone to slowly bleed to death.)

Suddenly he found himself moaning, an unrecognizable sound oozing out of him like thick liquid. It was an even flow, an inner weeping more terrifying than fear itself, for it could readily turn into a scream. A thunderous scream like an unexpected gush. But the weeping petered out and he realized that he lacked the strength even to open his mouth and reveal himself.

"Hello, hello. Do you remember telling me that you wrote in order not to die? But I've just discovered, and it's horrible, that I am dying in order not to write."

"Agustín, stop it. If you don't want me to come to your place, then you come here. Come and we'll talk."

Agustín was surprised to find it so late at night when he finally went outside. But what night? It seemed like the same one but wasn't, of course, this one already charged with intimations of the other one.

Roberta had some warm soup waiting for him, which he rejected with intense, inexplicable revulsion. But he ate the entire loaf in the breadbasket, drank wine, and nibbled at the cheese, though he kept insisting, I'm not hungry, can't swallow a thing. Roberta stared at him with mounting desperation, trying to figure out what had happened in the last few days in Agustín's life to upset him so. She couldn't for the moment raise the question; whatever had happened seemed too intense to serve as reply to a simple query.

And so Roberta remained silent, not at all typical of her, who always burst out with questions and demands at the slightest provocation. Instead, feelingly, disgustingly domestic, she fixed him a cup of herbal tea, allowed him to stretch out on the bed in his clothes, and lay down beside him only when he beckoned with a barely perceptible gesture.

Agustín hugged her desperately for a long while, and she did nothing to loosen his arms or to break free. She let him release what preyed upon him, understood that in squeezing her he was freeing himself gradually of a pressure of unsuspected magnitude. Crushed by Agustín's body, she could scarcely breathe and all the ghosts of childhood began assailing her, the despair of those days when her older cousin would try to smother her with a pillow and sometimes came close to it. But not Agustín—with Agustín it was different: he was the vulnerable one, he the one in despair.

After a while Agustín muttered, No, no, and curled up against the wall, resting only one hand on Roberta's hand. And so much electricity coursed through those hands, such a current of things unsaid, that the No was transformed into a Yes, yes, and Agustín felt that never had he been so close to Roberta, so much with her in the midst of pleasure; an inexplicable pleasure considering the circumstances, a total surrender when in reality what he should have done was to encyst his senses, for they had driven him into the heart of terror.

Agustín opened his eyes at dawn and in that dim, quivering light saw Roberta's anxious eyes searching for some clarification.

"No," he said for the second or perhaps hundredth time that night.

"No," she answered drowsily, because she was barely awake, because she had not prodded him. "I don't need any words, either written or spoken, nothing. We were so close last night."

Roberta's total acceptance weakened Agustín's defenses. And Agustín confessed. At least he partially confessed, disguising reality so as not to offend Roberta, or perhaps just to keep her at his side:

"I killed a man."

And Roberta, bewildered, didn't wince or say, You're crazy. She scrutinized him more intently than before, and he sensed that she believed him, and thanked her in silence. Then he was able to proceed.

"The other day I killed a man, and the worst part is I don't know why."

"And how did you do it?"

"I shot him," he said, barely audible, but also as if recounting someone else's story. "I shot him in the temple."

"Agustín, you're ranting. A bullet. At whom? And where would you get hold of a pistol?"

And I bought the revolver to take to the house in the Adirondacks, remember? I told you the place was very isolated and that I needed protection, but I was positive I'd never get to use it, it was only to have the security of a weapon, a shot into the air if it became necessary, just that—and now look. No, he didn't attack me. Nothing like that. I had that damned revolver less than a day and wound up shooting it—at a head, the head of a poor wretch I'd never seen in my life."

"A gun with a mind of its own. Like the daggers in Borges stories."

"He was a stage actor. I saw him in a play."

"An actor? Is this some kind of comedy?"

"No. A tragedy. A real one, not my imagination. No, it isn't my imagination, unfortunately. I killed him for real and it seems like a dream."

"Maybe it'll turn out that it *was* a dream. A nightmare. You have to consider that possibility. It happens—you see it in literature. You've read Sontag."

"Yes, thank you. I've also read Camus, and Gide, the gratuitous act, all that. But this ain't literature, baby, this is sheer truth. When I kill, I kill. Or at least I killed, this one and only hallucinated time. Not reading, not writing. Killing."

"Cut it out, man. Why kill someone you don't even know?"

"If I knew why, I'd turn myself in to the police. Or better yet, I would never have killed in the first place. Imagine. I'm not the sort who goes around taking justice into his own hands, I'm not a violent man. I don't know why I killed, and that's the worst of it. When I learn why, at least I'll be able to know who I am again, even though I'm sentenced for murder."

Roberta allowed a pause to elapse, which Agustín found worse than if she had pushed him away from her. But after what seemed like the briefest of naps—a catnap, as it were—entailing in fact an examination of her own feelings, devoid of any logic, Roberta said, "You can count on me. I don't know how, but I'll try to help you find out. Tell me how it happened."

"I'm exhausted. Let me sleep a little more, and then I'll tell you everything. Let me pull myself together."

"You don't have to tell me anything right now, just what you did with the revolver."

"I don't know. I don't know. My head hurts me so—as if I were the one who'd been shot. Everything must be smeared in blood."

Roberta's initial response to Agustín's story was not one of interrogation but of concealment. First priority: to find the weapon used in the alleged crime and get rid of it. With that in mind she took the precautions Agustín had implored her to take. She got to his apartment at precisely nine-thirty A.M. in order to slip in between the time when people left for work and the mailman's arrival. She made herself virtually invisible so as not to arouse suspicion—as if anyone were in charge of anything in that building of rickety steps and dark halls. She recalled a certain evening last summer when, climbing those same steps she'd come to an abrupt halt, bumping into a guy behind her: Sorry, I almost stepped on a cockroach. Welcome to New York, he'd said with a shrug, and Roberta had understood, and now here she was once again, again recognizing the city with that feeling of welcome to other dark omens.

Before opening the door, trying as instructed not to make any noise—the reverse of his act on closing another door—she wondered what to do with Sunday's newspaper, a telltale sign of Agustín's absence. Best to remove it. Anyone could have stolen it. A missing newspaper proves nothing.

Up until that moment Roberta had managed to retain her composure. But no sooner did she open the door and enter the apartment than the world around her collapsed. She realized then that Agustín had indeed told the truth. His innermost, dreadful truth. And she felt herself drowning.

First there was the stench. The putrid smell of that room like a solid, palpable presence in the dimness. She forced herself to close the door behind her, to prevent the smell from wafting through the halls, announcing the disaster.

Then she had to pass through the fumes to reach the window, like someone allowing herself to be licked by the most noxious of tongues. She drew or rather ripped the curtains aside and opened the window top and bottom—to allow a bit of air, of so-called reality, to dispel the miasma.

The stench was readily dispelled. A mere current of air and a brief wait while she contained her nausea. But the nausea lingered; no breeze could dispel it as long as she remained in that polluted room.

It was here that Agustín's guts had turned inside out like a glove; his physical despair pervaded sight, smell, touch.

Roberta sat down on the edge of the bed and wept with muffled sobs, swallowing the wail she would have liked to let loose on that very spot, lying on Agustín's repugnant sheets. She could not guess that he, in her bright apartment, was also weeping. Because from inside Roberta's wastepaper basket, Edwina's eyes were condemning him.

He was able to cry only a little. As if all the liquid of his body had been depleted—a dry, brittle body that would crumble at his very first step. Which he took. He went to the wastepaper basket, knelt devoutly, lifted out the *New York Post,* and clipped the photograph from the first page. But he lacked the strength to even read the headline or to turn to the page with the story. All he could do was cut out that face, isolating the eyes and nose and mouth, keeping only Edwina's features stripped of everything that had given her human semblance. Then he slipped the clipping into an inner fold of his wallet, where he imagined keeping it forever.

Roberta meanwhile recovered sufficiently to enter the bathroom, empty the Lysol bottle into the tub and turn on the faucets all the way. Purification and cleansing. Then she put the towels and sheets into a big paper bag, thinking it would be safer to throw them in the garbage than take them to the laundry.

The raincoat, which had been rolled into a ball on the floor, got properly hung on a hook in the bathroom. The other clothing was gathered and piled in a corner, the bedspread laid out on the bed.

With the restoration of a certain order Roberta regained a sense of command. And finally, after much going back and forth, amid a fit of tidiness that prompted her to rearrange the desk in the other room, she forced herself to pick up the jacket thrown on the chair and to examine it. It was a rust-colored tweed and appeared to have no bloodstains, though it was hard to be certain. Almost timidly she stuck her hand into the right-hand pocket. And found the gun.

It was more than she could bear, yet consoling. Agustín wasn't mad after all, at least not totally out of his mind. Better to think him a murderer than victim of some awful hallucination. Better reality, atrocious as it was, than to see him permanently installed in that realm we aspire to only as rather dispassionate spectators. While saying this to herself, pointing the revolver toward the bed as one sees in movies, she cracked the cylinder and removed the bullets. One was missing. She weighed the bullets in her hand and, without too much deliberation, flushed them down the toilet.

"I think I did what had to be done. Cleaned up the place. Collected sheets, towels, and other junk into a bag and dumped it in a garbage pile, far from the house. I also threw out the shirt, just in case, though it didn't seem stained. A maroon shirt—not that it matters. The jacket looked fine and I hated to throw it out."

"And the revolver?"

"I took care of that, too. There are no traces left."

"No traces? Certain traces are impossible to erase."

"One does what one can. Anyhow, I speak for myself. What one can. I also bought you some shaving stuff. I think it'll make you feel better."

"I've had a beard for almost twenty years. It even survived the dictatorship, when you had to shave for your documents. I've hardly ever seen my bare face."

"You'll see it now. You'll have to if you want to go out into the world. And you do, don't you? You want to find out what actually happened, don't you?"

"Yeah, I want to know everything. Why it happened, why me, everything. But I don't know what the beard has to do with all that."

"I don't want you to be recognized. You'll act more freely if you feel different. Like another person."

"Enough of that nonrecognition crap. I feel so lost, and now you're going to change my looks."

"I'm not changing anything. You're the one making the

change, and you'll be yourself, with or without a beard. You might also put on eyeglasses."

"I see perfectly well. I didn't do what I did because of faulty eyesight."

"I brought you the glasses recommended for resting your eyes. It would be a good idea to wear them all the time. You'll get used to being clean-shaven, to wearing glasses, to looking like someone else in order to find yourself, know what I mean?"

Baby's rump, said Roberta, stroking his smooth cheek. The shaving ceremony had been long and rather sad. Like a farewell. First with scissors, then lots of lather, an old-fashioned safety razor, plenty of swearing, a slight cut—and baby's rump, but a baby that's been sunbathing with its diapers on, Roberta added, in part to hide her disappointment at the sight of a rather weak jaw and a receding chin.

"I never sunbathe, you know, with or without diapers."

"You'll have to now, sweetie, 'cause there's no better corpus delicti than that map face of yours. We'll put some tanning lotion on you, and out you go to the balcony to bask in the smile of Phoebus."

She tried to get him to put on an old pair of her shorts, but her powers of persuasion faltered. I'll have to ask Ava for help, she thought, get her to come with the whip or whatever she uses to dominate men. But who knows, maybe I could have a go at it myself—might come in handy, she thought, but not today. Kid gloves are doctor's orders for the sufferer today.

And what about that other man, the one who suffered because of him? The one, that is, whose life he took without any suffering at all, without so much as saying, Here goes? That person no longer exists, never did exist for Roberta, and would materialize only when investigations, the inquest, began. She would have to check the papers, find out who he was, what could possibly have prompted Agustín to do what he did. A gay squabble? Not unlikely. Some gay accepted or rejected, denied or resisted, flagrantly or by insinuation, consciously or unconsciously. What a mess. She'd have to investigate on her own, check out secret motivations and other stuff, but not yet. All that mattered now was trying to resurface to a life devoid of vomit, of spilled blood and other slime.

She settled Agustín on the balcony in her only folding chair, handed him a glass of nicely chilled white wine, and went in to prepare a snack. Then she brought out the tray, a small wicker chair for herself, another glass, and some chitchat about old times. As if that were possible.

Agustín with his face to the sun.

Hateful. Who? The sun. It's your friend today, not too hot, October already. True, but still.

And gazing down at the street, from eight stories up, fortunately with no one opposite to spy on them, only the terrace of a health club across the way where people were earnestly jogging around the track or playing tennis, as if that's what life were all about, as if life were not taking the life of someone else. Or waiting for someone to come and take yours, in reprisal.

The two of them were thinking the same thoughts but were reluctant to express them. They confined themselves to gestures, a pained expression, careful not to utter an incriminating word in light of those interconnected balconies, in this city that has become dangerously bilingual.

"How's the novel coming?" Roberta finally asked, breaking a heavily charged silence.

"You know. At a standstill. I can't write, nothing comes out of me, now less than ever."

"I'm not talking about your old novel. I mean the one you began on Friday."

"Oh, that. It isn't a novel. It's a play. A tragedy, if you re-member."

"Tell me about it."

"I can't, it's still too raw. And I need the setting, the stage set, the three usual walls plus the invisible fourth. The nonexistent wall is the one I need most, to lean on. There's also a man—"

"A dead man."

"No, don't even remind me of him. Another one, a live man, out there, who on a certain shadowy night gives the protagonist, or rather, the antagonist, the antihero, a theater ticket."

"And why does the antihero accept it?"

"Because he's a jerk. Because he's an enlightened soul, a dharma bum. Because he had nothing else to do and was poking into prohibited zones. Because maybe that was his terrible fate, his destiny. Because in his youth he read *Steppenwolf*. Because he reads Cortázar and Bataille. Because he doesn't know what reading, much less writing, is. Because everything is theater and he'd just as soon walk through the grisly streets as stick himself in a dark playhouse. Because he loves Artaud. Because he has no sense of humor. Because he has a mad sense of humor. Because he is mad. Because—"

"Cut it out. The protagonist or antihero or whatever doesn't need to know his motives. But you do. As an author, I mean."

"I'm not the author of anything."

"You're the author of the deed."

Roberta went to get the wine she'd left in the fridge. She did want to unravel the whole business, but not that much. Another glass of wine. Yes, thank you. Some more tuna, some palmetto with mayonnaise? Just like back home, but the *golf* sauce is missing, the thousand island. Put some ketchup in the mayonnaise. Forget it, this play will be brimming with ketchup. Pass me a sliver of smoked mozzarella. Delicious with sage and olive oil. Another sip of wine, the pleasures of the idle.

"It would be nice to get away while the weather is good, maybe to Cape Cod."

"I don't want to run away. For once, I don't want to run away. I've got my tragedy going, don't forget."

"You don't forget you've got a substantial grant. It gives you what's needed most, time for research. To get your tragedy launched, that is. Do you have a title yet?"

"A title? No."

"We have to give it one. What do you think of *Friday Night*?"

"Awful. And not very original. I suggest the *The Scream*."

"What scream do you suggest?"

"*Basta,* gimme a break! *The Scream,* as a title. It's from Artaud, from *An Affective Athleticism* (get that!). 'The rest is done with screams.' "

"It reminds me of Munch's painting, too, a mouth open with horror, like a great void. I don't want a great void."

"I'll fill it for you. Roberta. One of these days, when I can, I'll fill it for you. I promise. But now I'm going inside. The void is oppressive."

Roberta got furious. Was he starting again with his empty promises? She gazed at his face, already getting pink in its less exposed areas, and felt like throwing her glass of wine at him. Or at least the wine, with a quick flick of her wrist. Agustín guessed what she had in mind. Wine isn't a good suntan lotion, he said, rising to his feet, and both of them broke into spontaneous laughter, which united them on the brink of confrontation.

I am you and you are me. Whom did we kill? The assertion remained; the question drifted off through the air of that balcony suspended too far above nothingness.

They kept gazing into each other's eyes up there for a long while, without further understanding but with mounting desire, that crafty little bird.

Gazing at each other, gazing without saying a word. Agustín was the first to reach out his hand. Come, he said softly, and either she didn't hear him or she preferred to remain where she was, still looking at him, trying to understand something.

Come, come, he insisted. A beckoning that wedged open doors clamoring to remain shut.

Agustín, nice and clean, freshly bathed—by Roberta—wearing a pair of Roberta's jeans and one of her T-shirts, his smooth-shaven cheeks and chin flushed from the autumn sun, his hair tousled (let's face it, *porteño,* your hair is wavy—why bother slicking it down?), and a pair of glasses jammed on his nose.

"I feel comfortable like this."

"Sure, it's you. Why always wear a tie, all buttoned up?"

"It's not that, woman."

"I think we're ready for act two. The street calls us."

The sun was going down as they headed toward the Lower East Side, the ambiguous Loísa whose jaws a few days ago had opened to swallow Agustín. Their aim was to backtrack, to see if they could pick up any clue. There's a Moroccan restaurant near Avenue A that looks good, Roberta suggested, as if to muffle the fear of returning to the scene. I hate . . . Agustín had begun saying, though he never finished, Arab dishes. Just then he realized that the moment had arrived for crossing boundaries, donning a new skin, acquiring new tastes, and so he left the I hate floating between them in midair without separating them, as a token of assertion, a sign of the little he had left. He'd even left his name behind. No longer would he be called Agustín, but from now on would be Gus or, because of his glasses, Magoo. One more form of protection and concealment in case other members of the audience at the underground theater had heard his name.

I am Agustín Palant, was the first thing, it seems, he had told his victim-to-be, and Roberta on learning this insisted on giving him a nickname, choosing from a reasonable range of variations.

I am—was—Agustín Palant, he'd said aloud in the middle of the theater, and thus it had become essential to eradicate Agustín Palant, barely leaving his caricature.

Very soon Agustín—sorry, Magoo—began feeling the relief of those transformations. Moreover, right from the start he'd referred to the victim in neuter form. *Victim*, until the word became intolerable and they began calling him/her just plain Vic, with a touch of sadistic triumph that neither acknowledged.

Vic. A creature utterly unknown to him, having materialized in a theater over a steaming pot of soup—a totally anticlimactic situation that might or might not crop up again in another act.

In this second act there are only two protagonists, who have set out to reconstruct another scene: Magoo's stroll after purchasing a weapon and before shooting said weapon. Their goal is to find the theater, the scene where the drama unfolded that would lead to tragedy. Fearfully, with great trepidation, they look for it. Which makes them feel somewhat heroic.

It is approximately the same hour of twilight, when things have lost the precision of daytime and haven't yet yielded to the false contours of night. The hour might be identical, but the atmosphere is quite different. This vast midweek plateau isn't the same as the Friday evening dividing line, and Magoo no longer recognizes his terrain. I think he turned the corner about here, he says, referring to himself in the third person, trying to split from Agustín and be just Magoo, narrator of the story. Except, when it comes to the story, Magoo knows as much or even less about it than Agustín, probably less because he is entering the winding path of someone reciting only half-truths, who at every turn fibs a tiny bit more and in saying Vic tries to imagine a man, even though it was a woman. Whereupon everything becomes unexpectedly transformed, forcing him away from his memories.

"I think he went into this seedy bar, ordered a beer and hung around watching some Puerto Ricans shooting craps."

"Let's go in then. Order some beer."

"No, not again."

"Yes, if you want to know. Yes, if you mean to discover the motive."

It was in and out in a split second. All glances were glued on Roberta, down to her very skin. Not here, said Agustín, in English to throw them off. Not where the dangerous ones are the others.

"We have to find the one who gave you the ticket."

"It was my intention, but I doubt if I'd recognize him. And anyhow, I won't have the nerve to approach him."

"That's another story. I can do that, to learn something. But try, try to remember what he looked like, some particular feature, something."

"I just don't know."

So little ground covered, and already they felt exhausted.

They sat down on a park bench, for there was still a glimmer of light outside. A bench hugging the street, of course, not daring to penetrate this no-man's-land.

"What a lark! Just look at us, scared, cautious, pussyfooting around the jaws of the wolf when actually I'm the one to be scared of. That's the one both of us should fear. Agustín, that is, Agustín the wolf. Why be scared of tame dogs at twilight?"

"Don't overdo it, Gus, Magoo. The world and Tompkins Square are filled with wolves."

"Gus, Magoo, Gog and Magog. Look what I've turned into."

"Now that we're nicely seated with the howling pack behind us, tell me all about the play. The play within our play, within the one we're now writing with the body. Go on, tell me. Who was Vic? The main character?"

"No, but with a part that I found very enticing. Moving, I'd say. Don't know why. Can't even seem to remember the play. Do you really think it's worth pursuing this?"

"No. We can leave everything just as it is. How about it? 'Me, Argentine'; dish out our typical remarks: 'Nothing has happened here,' or, 'They must have done something to deserve this.' "

"Cut it out. You're really bugging me."

"Okay. Another possibility—we can take off calmly for the country. Or Paris. What do you think? Or you can go back to our dear old Buenos Aires and be off the hook. We'll correspond from time to time, you sending me postcards of the obelisk and I answering with a bit of news, anything I can dig up. If you're still interested."

"Get to the point."

"The point is I don't think anyone's after you. You're one in two hundred million, dig that. Hop the next plane to Buenos Aires, and on with the show. Not that I want you to go. Quite the opposite. Nor can I get you to stay. But you've got money from your grant. Use it."

"Lay off. I'm tied hand and foot. I have my conscience, and there's the rub. Besides, having killed one person, I just might at an off moment kill another—considering I don't even know why I did it, and didn't even realize I was doing it."

"You have no gun now."

"That's the least of it. Better that I don't, but where did you put it?"

"My business. Don't worry. C'mon, let's get going."

Roberta had hidden the revolver in her apartment for several reasons, the first and main one being that she'd never worked up the necessary courage to stick it in her handbag again and go outside to throw it away somewhere. She had plenty of plans. Her favorite scenario unfolded along the Hudson River: In her hand was a paper bag, from which she drew an apple and ate it. Then she tossed the bag into the water. Too loaded a sandwich, she might explain to some casual observer as the bag sank with the revolver stuck between two slices of innocent white bread.

The gun, tucked behind rows of jars in the medicine chest, was indeed a heavy presence. Every once in a while Roberta would take it out of its hiding place to make sure it was still unloaded (one mustn't forget, she said to herself, that it's the devil himself who loads guns) and to polish it once again in a desperate attempt to erase Magoo's slightest fingerprint. She cleaned it over and over, just in case she'd missed some crevice. And should the police by chance arrive to search the house, she could always say that the revolver was hers. And it was true, now that she'd appropriated it without telling Magoo where it was. But of course, if the police came to her house, it was because Magoo was under suspicion, and then everything would be lost.

All this reasoning did not free her from her gun-polishing obsession. And even less from another, much more disturbing one: checking to make sure that the gun was still in its hiding place after each of Magoo's visits to the john.

"It was at this corner, I think it was this corner where I was given the ticket. Actually not. I don't remember this grocery store—the *grocería,* as it's called around here. C'mon, we'd better go, don't you think? I'm sure I'll never recognize the guy with the ticket. A black, I think, light; maybe an Arab. If people only knew what was in store for them, they'd look more carefully. Besides, the city is full of blacks of different shades and they all look alike."

"What do you mean they look alike? There are blacks and blacks. Some are really gorgeous, so don't give me that."

"You know. I don't notice men."

"No? How about Vic?"

"Vic is something else. Belongs to the theater. Vic is, or was, playing a role. Vic isn't a person. If Vic showed up, I don't think I would recognize the face."

They were moving away from the spot, in any event, but Roberta took note of the corner: the grocery, a funereal florist across the street, and a dark doorway where you'd catch junkies shooting up or creeps selling kiddie-porn, to say nothing of guys handing out tickets that poison the soul. At some point she'd return on her own, looking like someone wanting to go to the theater with unspeakable intentions.

Magoo nudged her to speed up.

"Let's go home."

"Your place or my place?"

"I don't have a place anymore, don't you know that? I'm now barely a bullet lodged in a skull."

Roberta didn't bother to answer Better a bullet in a skull than a bullet gone astray. He didn't look in a mood for jokes, and besides, the joke had an edge of cruelty—infinitely better to be a bullet gone astray, a shot in the air. She told him none of this, but decided that somehow the air of gloom had to be dispelled. Other paths would have to be explored if they truly wanted to clarify something. And she was ready. And felt a certain exaltation in it all. Look at him, she said to herself, look at the meticulous, precise jerk, now mired in the chaos of death. More than ever she wanted to shake Agustín, to break down the wall, force him to reveal himself—to rebel against himself?

Therefore she insisted on going into the antique-clothes store, where the bric-a-brac was redolent of lavender and mothballs.

"As long as we're changing appearances, Magoo, let's change our clothes—seek redress, as they say."

They had been rummaging for a long while in silence, elbow-deep in piles of clothing that smelled of grandma's attic—assuming one had a grandma with an attic and stuff like that—then began wandering off in other directions, fingering crystal goblets, picking up a lamp from the twenties that would go well with the dress Magoo had chosen for Roberta. Roberta had just shoved Magoo inside the fitting room, which was actually a Persian rug suspended like a curtain between two clothes racks, when out of the martial depths of tulle and tattered silk curtains came the roar of a machine gun.

"Roberta, ta ta ta-ta ta!"

The way Roberta jumped was worthy of being recorded on video, as the instigator would later remark. What no video would have revealed was Magoo's anxiety in front of the huge mirror—Venetian, of course—trying on a ridiculous greenish outfit chosen by Roberta, feeling entrapped.

"Lara, queen of absurdity, it's you. You nearly scared me to death!"

"Roberta, princess of metalinguistics, who else but me would you find in a place like this?"

"Is this shop yours?"

"Might as well be. Monique, the owner, is a close friend. If you come tonight after eleven, I'll introduce you. She's only here at those hours; her favorite clients come after the theater. They are the loonies, the defeated, the merciless, the others. What are you looking for?"

"Theatrical costumes, of course. I'm with a friend who's writing a play. Pure theater of cruelty, you know. He's a worthy disciple of Artaud."

"Doctor's orders. Come over one of these evenings and see how lovely my place looks now. I changed the entire decor, you'll love it, and besides, I want you to meet some divine friends who live upstairs. I'll call you. Have to run—there's a van outside waiting for me. I just came to get a pair of dressmaker dummies I desperately needed for my decor. Bill is going to help me load them, aren't you? That's Bill, there in back, Monique's partner. This is Roberta, a lady of Latin American letters—you should be friends. Don't you adore this old mannequin? I swapped it with Monique for a fabulous door I found the other day at a demolition site. But I needed these bodies, I've got perfect heads to go with them. Okay, I'll call you. I promise."

Agustín felt he couldn't stand it anymore inside the mirror-lined fitting room and surfaced for air just at the moment they were taking the second mannequin outside. He saw a body covered with a blanket and had the sensation that it was Edwina's body being carried out. He wanted to run out of the shop, and Roberta couldn't convince him to stay one minute longer, even to collect what she had chosen.

"Could it have been Bill who gave you the ticket?"

"The thought occurred to me, but no. That's not why I wanted to run out of there. I had the feeling they were taking out a body, and it stirred up so many images from other times. Buenos Aires, you know. But it was someone else who gave me the ticket, someone not even black, perhaps, some other skin color, like I said. That's all I remember."

By now they had slackened their pace, on the safe side of things once they had crossed First Avenue. They were strolling, hands linked, and Roberta felt a tenderness surge from the soles of her feet, creep gently along her legs, and engulf her.

Agustín was holding her hand like a child and Roberta was

beginning to feel reconciled with the world, when a sudden memory made her let go of his hand, with rage. It was not the thought of what he was capable of doing with that hand but the reminder of what he was incapable of doing: giving it. It was as if she had been struck by the train the two of them were traveling on together some time back, when her head was hurting so badly she reached for Agustín's hand for consolation. He kept it there barely half a second, then withdrew it with a muttered rejection. I don't like having my hand grasped, I feel trapped, he'd said. And Roberta had begun to cry inconsolably. Later she'd tried to understand what it was all about, telling herself that he, having lost his mother at the age of two, was barely acquainted with affectionate hands, only hands that seized him to drag him to places where he didn't want to go. Of course, Roberta's hand, that time on the train, was filled with other intents, with not the slightest intention of trapping him or leading him. But he had withdrawn his hand, and now he was clinging to hers in a reversal of roles.

She brought Agustín back to her house nonetheless and fixed him a hot bath sprinkled with herbs.

"What are those leaves floating in the water?"

"Well, rosemary for muscular tension and headache. And mint, which is a tranquilizer. You'll see, it'll do you good. Get in and take as much heat as you can, like a hot tub."

"You're nuts, woman, I'm going to feel like boiled beef in that caldron of broth. The only thing missing are cannibals dancing around."

"I'll dance if you want."

"The *vagina dentata* to the beat of the tom-tom."

"It has no teeth, it's about time you found that out."

"No? Look what you're doing to me now, sticking me in soup. Remember—have some consideration."

"You're the one who needs to remember. After all, it may be a good idea, the soup. You may need to immerse yourself in a proper culture to see clearly. To understand, and then to write.

There's the typewriter, paper, lots of pencils, everything you need. Use my pen, I'll lend it to you, you'll break the barrier right away. Blocked material, as some of our acquaintances would say."

"And you, where are you going?"

"I'm going shopping. To buy some food."

"You're leaving me alone? Aren't you going to bathe me?"

"I'm leaving you alone for just a little while. So that you'll concentrate."

She sat on the couch waiting for Agustín to get out of the tub. Agustín called her in, to help him get dry. Roberta decided not to play mother now, or any of those different games they might have played.

She waited for him to come out of the bathroom, loaned him her bathrobe, and placed him in front of the desk. Try at least to write something, jot down what you remember about the play you saw. I would've liked to see it too—maybe the plot will give us a clue.

"It had no plot, nor do I remember the play. There were lots of characters going back and forth. Shouting, dragging a flag. And one guy who went around hauling an ancient typewriter which he used at times as a platform. I think he represented Brecht, it sounded like Brecht. Anyhow, let's drop the subject."

"Maybe I'll go over to the theater and check it out."

"Don't go. Please, do me a favor and don't go."

Roberta put on her coat, grabbed her handbag.

"As you like. I'm not going to butt into that reality if you don't want me to, but we ought to be sure that there is a reality behind all this. Make sure that there is a corpse, even if it's in the closet. I won't go butting into your reality, but I can bring you some elements so that you can enter it without too many risks. Me, I can stay calm on this side of the metaphor—anyway it's your metaphor. You're the one who has to transcend it."

"Don't remind me, don't remind me," Agustín lamented.

And when he was alone, he climbed into bed and covered his head.

As expected, Roberta tried to return to the scene of the crime, but not knowing exactly where that was, she wound up in the vintage clothes store to pick up a dress she'd seen and a black jacket that Magoo had tried on.

Bill smiled as though he'd been waiting for her.

"I heard you two say you were going to put on a play. Can you use an actor?"

"You'd be just right for us," Roberta replied, and meant it. If the play were ever written and produced, Bill would be perfect for the role of the man who gives away the ticket, though Roberta would have preferred him as the victim. Yeah, Bill in the role of Vic and she playing the murderer. To get to know the feeling. No shooting in the head though—this handsome specimen had to be strangled with her bare hands.

"Yes," she went on. "There may also be a part in the play for me; it's open to all sorts of possibilities, the more challenging the better. If you know what I mean."

"I like that. I like you, too. Let's try on costumes."

"Sure. Today, I choose."

"Choosing is good. To be chosen is even better."

Roberta began rummaging in the piles of clothing and curtains, poked around among the racks and hangers, buried her arms in dusty lengths of lace. Bill hoisted himself up on the counter and sat swinging his long legs, smiling indulgently. Roberta, pulling out velvets and satins, discovered a velvet vest with

sequins for him. You're going to look like Othello, she said. But
you'll please me. Now me, what shall I wear?

Put this on, he said, thrusting his hand into a basket on the
counter and drawing out some red fabric. He threw the rags at
Roberta, catching her full in the face. Lookin' for a fight, are
ya? she challenged, and began flailing at him with what appeared
to be an evening gown. Bill jumped off the counter, roaring with
laughter, and hid behind an old phonograph with a horn and a
stack of acetate records. Roberta joined in the game and began
chasing him, not laughing, recalling Ava Taurel. I'll show you,
you wild beast! she hissed as she picked up the record on top
of the pile. She threw it like a discus and hit a lamp with a fringe
of beads, which began jingling. Bill snatched a green hat trimmed
with roses, jammed it on Roberta, then pulled it down over her
eyes. As she tried to pull it off, he jumped over a rattan coffee
table covered with curios. Roberta ran around the table, knocked
over a mannequin on the way, lunged at Bill, Bill grabbed her
without getting much resistance, just enough to keep the game
going, and together they fell onto one of the piles of garments
and assorted items. Roberta wrapped a shawl around his head,
he tried to tie her wrists with a feather boa.

They were laughing so hard they could barely move, when
two customers walked in and began looking around. They spotted Bill and Roberta while elbowing their way through the mess
and were on the verge of protesting or something, when Bill
managed to recover his voice and say We're closed. Okay, they
answered and left, swiping a cigarette case from among the
articles strewn on the countertop.

"Everything has its price," said Bill as he went to lock the
door.

"It's almost eleven. Your nocturnal mistress will be here any
minute."

"Today, ma'am, you're my mistress. But if you happen to be
referring to Monique, let me tell you she ain't no boss or mistress
of mine, and what's more, she's in Massachusetts hunting for

junk, as if we didn't have enough already. She's in Salem, I bet, pursuing her natural inclinations or poking around again in the abandoned puppet house. What a spooky joint!"

Whereupon he took off his shirt and jeans, and remained stark naked, splendid under the light of the silk-shaded lamps which brought out the sheen of his dark skin. All sorts of emotions and secretions were aroused in Roberta, who was still stretched out on the heap of clothing and entwined in swathes of lace, but Bill began getting into a pair of black tights.

"I'm not putting on that vest."

"Oh yes you are."

"I don't want to be Othello."

"Doesn't matter, you have to put it on."

"I'm a leopard." And he pulled on a silky black turtleneck. "A black panther."

"Okay," said Roberta. "In that case, I won't be Desdemona. Just as well." She peeled off yards of lace and proceeded to hunt for a long braided belt she had spotted near the entrance. "I always dreamed of cracking a whip," she said, attempting to brandish the belt, only to knock over a porcelain statuette that was missing an arm anyhow.

"Leopards can't be tamed."

"I'm a terrific tamer!" Roberta shouted, kicking her shoes a distance away like someone spitting, and groping around under an old armchair covered with shawls for a pair of spike-heeled boots she was sure she'd noticed somewhere.

"Les petites botines, les petites botines," she cooed softly, trying to sound like a character in a Buñuel movie. But getting into the charming boots—which she hoped were her size—was pointless, dressed as she was in a sweater and corduroy pants. No. Following Bill's example, she stripped, then cast around for something to put on. Quick, the sequined vest she had picked for him, quick a Manila shawl around her waist like a sarong. A Spanish broncobuster. *Olé!* This is my idea of great! shouted Bill as he leaped onto the counter. Whip, whip! he shouted, certain that she wouldn't get carried away and really light into

him, hard to do anyhow amid all that junk. And Roberta, tickled, squealing with laughter, wanting only to lash the floor and make Bill jump, to put a little fear into him, to whack the boards and have him jump to her beat. And Bill there, more than ready to jump, not for or because of Roberta but on top of her, and she not unyielding, yielded to the utmost, feeling ecstatic afterward and contrite at the same time for having been so unfaithful to Agustín. Unfaithful in the context of their quest.

"Bill," she said an hour or so later. "Bill, talk to me about the theater."

"Didn't you like ours?"

"I mean about the theaters in this area."

"It's packed with theaters. Secret theaters you couldn't even imagine. Theaters of sin and of sin against theater, the worst of all sins. Also, there's theater so utterly sublime that only a dozen people can watch it."

"Tell me about the others, what sins?"

"Whatever you want or can imagine. And that's not just a figure of speech. No kidding. You just tell them and they stage it for you."

"With oneself as protagonist?"

"If that's what you want."

"Do you mean anything goes, anything, anything?"

"Yep."

"Even killing a person?"

"Yes, if you can pay the price."

"And if you can't?"

"Then no. Unless someone else pays to watch you kill."

"**A**nd I also brought you this lion mask, this king of the jungle, to give you the courage to go outside, and a ski mask in case the other seems a bit too much."

"Thanks. Getting arrested for disorderly conduct—that's all I need."

"This is New York, baby. Nobody's out policing stuff like that. These streets are a circus, imagine if they arrested people for disorderly conduct. Gimme a break! There'd be no one out on the loose. Please, the jails are jammed, just remember that: the jails are jammed."

"You made me shave off my beard, toasted me to a turn in the sun. Now you want to cover up all the sacrifices I've made. King of the cement jungle. You'll make me more paranoid than I am, taking advantage of my defenselessness. I'll never be able to go outside again. Leave me alone!"

Roberta shut herself up in the bathroom. She had gone too far—there are things you can't play games with even if you want to. Are there? He had played, and contrary to what might be assumed, he had lost. She turned on the bathtub faucets, more to calm herself than to prepare a bath. She wasn't with someone who had hallucinated a crime. She was with a criminal, a victim of some dark, obscure script. Unwittingly he'd been placed on a stage and given the most dangerous role.

Magoo as the real vic. And Vic, who was that? Agustín's dark side? If only it were that easy. If someday on the street, in a movie house or a theater, we were to run smack into the person

who is our other part, the part we find intolerable to even acknowledge, and then bang! Could suppress it just like that without too many snags. What a relief. But Magoo isn't relieved,
he's tenser than ever, if possible, and maybe the whole thing was
a mistake and the other guy should have killed him, the other
guy should have killed this dark part of himself and been left
glowing, lighthearted.

And she, whom would she kill? What would the other, mur-
derable Roberta be like? Would she, the other one, write? Sup-
posing the other were prowling around at this very moment to
kill her? Maybe edging right now toward her door along the
carpeted hallway, silent as usual and more than fascinating.

Roberta at least could defend herself. Way up there in the
upper cabinet, Magoo's revolver was waiting for her.

Magoo was asleep when she slipped into bed alongside him.
Maybe pretending to sleep, but it didn't matter. Roberta turned
off the light and snuggled up to him, trying to fall asleep too
but managing only an anxiety-ridden half-sleep.

"Do you remember when we would get into bed and just fall
asleep? Do you know how to do that?"

Agustín didn't, he wasn't sleeping.

"I'm a sonofabitch, dragging you down in fear. Fucking sel-
fish—I've no right to do that."

"Forget it. I've joined the dance, and you know I like to dance."

Fear is the least of it, thought Roberta. He's putting me in
danger, and maybe I like danger more than dancing, more than
anything. I like other things, too, and feel it's essential to go
back and see Bill, and ask him some questions. He said that one
can get to kill if someone else is paying, paying for you to kill,
to watch you kill. To watch you kill. To watch Magoo the sur-
reptitious. Agustín. Saint Augustine. No, Saint Thomas. Seeing
is believing, there must have been a witness, a voyeur, an on-
looker who served as witness. The Great Spectator, feeling himself omnipotent and Agustín the puppet. There is always another.
An outside eye that gets you in a mess, into the hay. The haystack.

And the needle, where is that? Too many questions. *Basta*. Better not to discuss it with Agustín for the time being. Or allow him to stick his head again into the jaw of the wolf—always that idea, of the wolf, of not getting swallowed in its maw. Protect him. Probe the juicy mouth herself, investigate on her own, trying to understand, but to understand via the most circuitous paths, which are usually the only truly clarifying ones. Keep probing at the unconfessable, with a hand from Bill—no, not his hand, rather with Bill's tongue, with some word not always uttered. Riding horsie on Bill.

Half asleep, in that realm where one is simultaneously here and elsewhere, Roberta feels herself riding along gently in a rocking motion, which then becomes bumpier, like riding a camel. All around her is desert, endless dunes not burning but glittering under a cold lunar light. She too is lunar, transparent, almost happy behind the man riding the other camel. Or not. Now they are driving a modern jeep, her happiness tinged with fear. The man in the jeep is caressing her, murmuring tender words, but she knows that he's hiding something as they proceed amid dunes ever whiter and more iridescent—something stealthy yet conducive to just continuing on. Finally the cold awakens her, tears her from her lethargy. A window has blown open with the wind, and suddenly she's in her apartment, in her bed, and Agustín is tossing in his sleep, as he's been doing the past few nights—she'd been yearning for so long to have Agustín snugly at her side, and now that she has him, she's not sure she wants him. It's her house, it's her bed, and it's also her problem, as is the sudden understanding of the dream or reverie, particularly disturbing when awake. For she had once read about that, and thought it forgotten. Those things are never forgotten. Wealthy sadists in Cairo, Alexandria, or some other place at the desert's edge purchase everything, even a woman. Not prostitutes or slaves, or anything of the sort. Just beautiful women tourists ready for a good time. They travel alone, they are free and amenable to the idea of going to a party in the desert with some congenial sheikh ready to entertain them. To entertain them to the last drop, for the presumed sheikh has paid the pimp a substantial sum, and in the desert, where traces are immediately erased, the woman will be his to do with as he wishes, with impunity; and what he wishes is to kill her. Or to have her killed, as has been suggested.

Who has paid in this instance, and why? Who has collected, and how?

The expiatory victim is expiatory only when she knows her fate and yields to it with a kind of relief, accepting the idea, for she believes or intuits that she'll be transported to the other side and speak to the gods face-to-face.

The other women are mere victims, Vics, other instances of poor, not at all victorious Vic, whose name Roberta doesn't even know. Or want to know. If Agustín is a murderer, and of that she has no doubts—the man sleeping desperately by her side has committed a crime—if Agustín is a murderer and if she is seeking to help him illuminate his horror and at the same time to protect him, then she will try to tread only the areas demarcated by him, respecting his laws.

For the hundredth time, in another night that threatens insomnia, Roberta tells herself the story:

Man unexpectedly given ticket for dark theater. Said man identifies with a masculine character assigned the quite unmasculine task of preparing the soup, with much chopping of vegetables and steamy concentration. Not a chef, just a man taking the lid off the pot. And filling it, and bringing forth faintly scatological odors, boiled cauliflower. Then the other man, the spectator who was given the ticket, contrives to get himself invited to the soupmaker's house and without so much as a how-do-you-do, without stirring the broth, kills him.

With one point-blank shot.

Prompted by who knows what hidden motives if not by a backstage prompter. And the man who murders is Magoo, my Goo, Agustín Palant, silenced writer, allowing himself to be driven by his darkness, becoming thereby not so much mine as a strange Goo, property of his own victim, some goddamn fag. Or not. Try to understand as always, put yourself in his place, pry a wedge open. Don't get involved in hating, or killing in reprisal. Just suspend judgment for now and incorporate yourself in the story. Maybe all this has to do with love, ever mentioned love, somewhat over the edge.

"What did you do to yourself?"

"I left early and went to the beauty parlor, had my hair cut and dyed. Don't you like it? Do you think you're the only one who has a right to change his look?"

"Right—if only it were a question of right. What I have is an urgent need, and it's unbearable. *You* could have stayed as you were, without making fun of me."

"Forgive me. That's not what I meant to do. I did it out of solidarity."

"Ask me to forgive you again."

"Forgive me."

"I like you this way. You seem more fragile, less intimidating."

"What are you talking about? Me, intimidating?"

"Yes, with your dark, rebellious hair flying around. You seem tamer now."

"It isn't my hair but my soul that's dark and rebellious. Also my tongue, which has no hair, I assure you."

"You're telling me!"

It was past noon and Magoo was still in bed. The vertical position, linked to action, was becoming increasingly difficult for him, and only in Roberta's bed did he feel somewhat protected, preferably with Roberta alongside him. He drew her toward him, placed a finger in her mouth, and began probing around with great delicacy, looking for the hypothetical hairs on her tongue. At first Roberta surrendered to the delight of his touch, but then she rebelled, sensing it as a form of nonrecognition.

"You haven't said any more about my hair."

"I don't think this is the moment to worry about fashion."

"No. It's the moment for slipping into other skins."

And she didn't say dark skins, like Bill's, for that had not been her intention in going to look for him, early that morning, without the slightest hope of finding him in the store near Tompkins Square—eye of the tornado, vortex of the forlorn, where in the morning there were only creatures from other galaxies walking their dogs or the dopey masturbator wagging his long, limp dong to the beat of some mysterious inner music, making it flap like a banner, without the enthusiasm to bring it to life.

Past the Hell's Angels motorcycle park, past their metal-studded bikes and tattoo-studded biceps, was Bill's slumbering shop, and there, surprise of surprises, was Bill himself, slumbering on some velvet cushions with voile curtains serving as sheets.

Bill peered through the peephole to see who dared interrupt his dreams, and on seeing Roberta, opened the door and also his arms.

My beauty, he said. Forget it, she rejoined. I came for a sex change. I like that—here, you can have mine, he said, by an unmentionable path, so you'll become better acquainted with the other side of the coin. I don't care whether you like it, that's not why I came. Ah, bravo—I like that, too. You like everything, man, you're omnivorous. Sure am. Help me, I came for help, I have to get over to the other side. From above or below? he asked. Start from above. Your wish is my command, he said, and grabbed some scissors and snipped off a chunk of her hair. Since you've got nothing else to cut. Half the nape of her neck was left exposed. What a trophy! he shouted. Beast! she cried, I wasn't expecting all that.

"You can expect anything from me. You don't know me."

"No, I don't know you. But I'm getting to."

"That's what *you* think. Come, I'll cut the rest for you."

You're crazy. No, let me, it has to be evened out a little. You want my scalp—don't come near me. That's why you came. No.

The struggle, as was to be expected, led to something else. Later they went together to see Bill's friend on the next block, a barber, and Roberta wound up with clipped hair dyed Day-Glo orange. Bill liked the result and gave her the suit she was now wearing. A man's suit, of course, a number from the forties.

Of these rather brutal, impassioned transformations, only the results were obvious to Magoo. But he was the one who tried to rebaptize her, going along with the game. Robbie, he said, and then Bobbie, and with effort came up finally with Bob, pronouncing it like a bubble about to burst.

Roberta/Bob hadn't asked Bill more about people who pay to watch a murder or those who pay to be murdered, or other such aberrations. But Bill himself returned to the subject of the previous afternoon, asking her what the play was finally going to be about. Roberta recounted something very vague about a typewriter, one of those very old, heavy ones, which the leading character carts around on the stage. Bill gave her no feedback, nor did he put on a knowing look. The soup was not mentioned.

It had been a lot, too much for one single November morning. Roberta, Bobbie, Bob, Carrot-top, she'd had her fill of histrionics. Histrionics with lethal potentials, to boot. Ripping off the man's suit and tie, she tried to recover her skin, her name. Almost impossible, at this point. She ran to the bathroom, shut herself in—this was becoming a habit—and got under a steaming shower. But the fiery color didn't wash from her head, nor did her hair grow. And there, within arm's reach, was the hidden but shrill presence of the revolver, a violating weapon with which a man, her man, the one she'd thought she wanted to be her man, had despatched another man. It all came down to a matter of testosterone, a threshold she was unable to cross however much she tried to, even by shearing and transfiguring herself.

In the studio, one large undefined space, Agustín, too, was facing the unconfessable. From his wallet he had taken the newspaper clipping and, in his nakedness, was confronting Edwina's expression, the smile of his barely recognizable Vic, creased, smudged with sweat from his own hand, and he here in the raw, in the flesh, desperately wanting to but not allowing himself, lifting his free hand, moving it one step closer to transgression, but stopping as he hears the water and thinks of Roberta in the shower, Roberta as she was before all those stinking transformations.

To think, Roberta says to herself, that this shower curtain is a theater curtain now, and I'm stuck in this scene that isn't even mine. Stuck, despite myself, in the theater of cruelty, the theater of death. The death of another, the rending of love without even knowing whether true love exists, or where it belongs.

Roberta out of the shower now with the water still running, Roberta gazing at herself in the mirror, seeing herself so different, so close to the sinister edge of herself. And to think, and to think.

There is also a scene of the crime. If only she could get into that theater or into the apartment of the actor whom Magoo only mentions as Vic, not conveying whether, for him, the victim has or had a real name. Because Agustín is looking for the why of the act, whereas she'd like to know the where as well. One element connects her to the dazzling, terrible act: the weapon. She climbs onto the edge of the tub and gropes around the back of the top shelf of the medicine cabinet, searching among old bottles of forgotten drugs, till she finds the gun. Lethal like all those medicines kept out of negligence, which, since she no longer knows what they're used for or what they are, hence can become poisonous. Are poisonous. Another fascination to be pursued some other time. Now just stroke the revolver, transmitting to it her warmth and the warmth of that still-running water enveloping her in a mist. Hazy mirrors. But not the revolver, shiny under her caress, and though she knows that she herself unloaded it, you never know, she thinks. Slowly she moves it over her cheek, inserts the barrel in her mouth, and strokes the roof of her mouth as she had stroked Magoo earlier. Magoo meanwhile on the other side of the door is, unbeknownst to her, performing a ritual with Edwina's picture, or what remains of it, unable to pull himself together, to fathom it completely—just as he'd been unable to read the news item in the papers or extract concrete information.

The two of them on opposite sides of the bathroom door, unaware of each other, trying to find themselves along untrodden paths, probing into their own depths.

The fear of forlornness.

Agustín would like to keep that crumpled, fingered, splattered newspaper clipping forever, a mere tatter now on which only the eyes stand out. Roberta meanwhile knows that if she wants to protect Agustín and hence herself, she must dispose of the revolver one way or another. A potentially incriminating item in case Agustín should become suspect, or a collector's item in the more terrifying instance of the murder having been plotted by an infinitely powerful, perverse mind.

Roberta emerged from the bathroom, naked, looking utterly strange, alien. For the first time Agustín noticed how thin she had become or rather, how much weight she had lost. Her curves had melted away during those days of searching, and there before him stood what had once been Roberta, with raving red hair now, a very different person, neither helpless nor weak, androgynous.

She too viewed him differently and not just because the beard was gone and because he had a light, becoming suntan. Not even because he'd killed a man. It was something undefinable, kind of an air of satisfied gluttony, an air of that's-how-it-is-and-what-can-you-do. Also of revulsion. The cat that ate the canary—a forbidden, magical canary, like the fruit of the tree known to us all.

They gazed at one another and, naked, embraced. Or tried to embrace: the clutch of drowning swimmers.

Lovemaking had been out of the question for days, much less getting Magoo to respond favorably. But this time Magoo harbored a secret and was making headway.

"Come on. Keep up the spirit. You're getting there," Roberta whispered, more for his sake than hers.

"Does it matter to you much?"

"I don't know."

"Your indifference kills me."

"It isn't indifference, Magoo. It's perplexity."

(and better to kill than be killed, better to create order by trying to understand, but order is upsetting)

"It isn't indifference, Magoo, it's desperation. Despair."

He failed to understand. In some way he felt complete for the time being, completed, as if a cycle were closing. What he had done was done so unthinkingly that now he felt a strange satisfaction enveloped in nausea. An urge to vomit, the awareness that something could finally be regurgitated and thereby expelled from him. He didn't want to vomit it up, despite the nausea, and it was an induced nausea. It was his only way of assuming the deed, consuming it rather, for without realizing what he was doing, he had eaten Edwina's photograph bit by bit. Only newsprint but so much more. He'd begun by licking it, as if wanting to kiss it, and wound up sticking it all in his mouth and swallowing it. Edwina was now inside of him, imageless, sexless. Or not. Edwina all image, all sex, now part of him. Already rebelling.

Where does destruction end and appropriation begin? Where lies the secret memory of oblivion? Edwina—that image, the only thing left of her, and now there was nothing—Edwina still stirring up those unbearable memories, those other unbearable memories Roberta was totally unaware of, even if transmogrified, memories he himself was barely aware of, an entire country left behind, an era and a horror not labeled as such (screams in the house next door and desaparecidos). No. Unbearable memories of other victims who, like Edwina, would be mentioned no further.

Things that should never resurface, glimmerings of memory now muddling everything.

Roberta interrupted his silent ruminations, embracing him once more.

"Come, let's eat," she said. "There are other imperatives."

I know him so little, Roberta is saying to herself in the middle of the night, stroking him casually as he sleeps tense, unable to give in. I know him so little, and here I am trying to take care of him or perhaps absorb him like someone edging into another life, someone modeling herself on an image and likeness. I mean, without overdoing it.

She strokes him gently and in his dreams he doesn't purr but moans. Plaintive Palant. He murmurs something that sounds like yes in French. *Oui, oui.* Agustín, Roberta calls out, and he continues moaning. Come on, Magoo, wake up. No longer does he utter Edwina's name but he is filled with her. Death decanted and Magoo as good as dead.

"What's wrong, Agustín? Agustín, let's stop this game. Tell me the whole thing was a lie, everything just a stupid wish to write with the body. Tell me you were dreaming and I joined your dreaming."

"No."

"Then go back to B.A. Begin again. Start another novel. But a novel novel. Without theater, without doubles."

"Too late for that, kiddo. Let me sleep."

"And maybe I'll even go with you. We'll be respectable *porteños* again."

"Impossible. The place is branded. And so are we. Too many corpses there, as against just one here."

"You're crazy. The ones there aren't yours."

"They might as well be. We're all responsible. They're raking up corpses everywhere, from underneath the stones. It's unbearable. It's a city constructed over corpses, a nation of desaparecidos. There's no possible return."

"Escape."

"You know something? One cannot escape. You know, I'll stay but you can go."

'Yes. With flaming hair. I too am now branded."

"I don't want that."

"There are so many things one doesn't want. No. If I could at least know the dead man's face. Give me more details."

"You're asking for something else. Go to sleep. There's nothing I can give you, I have nothing."

"You do."

"No. Just a monstrous tiredness. Sleep. Think about your novel, about something else."

"You're my novel, now."

In the morning Roberta seems to have recovered her vital force despite her protruding ribs, and she dances for Agustín. With her hands Roberta tries Oriental undulations, which Agustín interprets as gestures of erasure, as if she wanted to eradicate those intimate memories of his which she doesn't share. The venetian blind is down but half open, and sunrays filter through the slats drawing a zebra pattern on Roberta's naked body. Roberta dances with mounting fury and Magoo timidly extends his hand to trap those stripes of light being distorted on her body, and his hand grows less timid, bolder, but the lines escape, fade away as Roberta's body is now here then gone, that warm, undulating, luminous, illumined flesh, a turn, a curve of the rump, a caress, a light slap, a grip. In frenzy. On the floor, Roberta! Crushed, as Magoo separates her legs. He opens her with his hands, wanting to tear her apart, but just opens her and penetrates her and crushes her, raises her legs into an impossible position and his elbow is jabbing into her shoulder, she can't free herself, nor does she want to, it's a pain that tunes into the pleasure, she submits to the pleasure with Magoo moaning as never before, releasing everything including the horror, an outcry that turns into a softer and softer, prolonged moan, until he breaks into sobs, Magoo stretched out, sapped, on top of Roberta, who is also sapped, in disarray, and happy.

They lie there stretched out on the carpet and something remains to be said, but it is not said.

"See, Bobbie, there are still men around."

"If you say so."

"I don't say so. I do so."

"Yeah, that's one way. I don't know, you hurt my arms."

"Forgive me. I have to relearn, looks like I still haven't relearned. I care for you, I don't want to hurt you. Neither you nor anyone else. I don't want to hurt anyone, you hear? And see what happened. I understand nothing, so how am I going to understand and accept you? You need a sensible man who won't hurt you."

"I don't need nothing when it comes to men. Don't give me that crap. The world is full of jerks saying the same thing, bunk about understanding and all that jazz. You at least have a right to say it, you went through an ultimate experience, you are justified.

"There are so many things you don't know about me."

"Right now I don't want to know them. I can't allow myself that supreme luxury."

"Nothing to know, everything to know. It doesn't matter. Let's change the subject—tell me about the novel you're writing."

"I already told you, my novel is the one we're writing together. The other one no longer exists. It's been erased, obliterated, contaminated because now it is part of all this crap. Or not. How to separate the wheat from the chaff? How to know where one begins and the other ends or vice versa? Life and the novel, I mean. How to explain the question of antennae and where one directs one's antennae in the need to capture, to appropriate everything out there that feeds and transforms the novel?"

"Cut it out, Roberta. It's too painful."

"I don't want to hurt you either, I just want to understand a bit, just a tiny bit. The novel, truth, which is which. The waters merge and cover us up."

"If only that were so, if only there were no distinction and a lead bullet were a paper bullet."

"And the reverse. We'd be indestructible. You realize that, Magoo, Agustín, Vic—Vic because you too are the victim and I shouldn't be telling you that. We could defend ourselves with the written word but that's not possible, the printed word smudges everything. Magoo, Magustín, the printed word, what a crummy aspiration. We have no other. Why don't you forget the shot that backfired and go back to your writing?"

"Because the shot exists and my writing doesn't. I don't mix things up as you do. I just know, and suffer."

"We're losing our sense of humor, Magustín, the last thing to be lost, after hope. Just think of what guilt you're trying to atone for, and why you're demanding such punishment."

"Mind your own business. I should never have come near you. Pouring salt on the wound. Leave me alone."

ROBERTA: I'm afraid the play we're planning is beginning to have political overtones.

BILL: Why do you say that?

ROBERTA: I don't know. Something I sniff in the air. It wasn't there before, and now—

BILL: You Latin Americans—

ROBERTA: You ethnic minorities shouldn't disavow these truths.

BILL: I don't. Tell me.

ROBERTA: I don't really know.

BILL: You don't know what?

ROBERTA: Anything. I don't know anything about the protagonist or the antagonist.

BILL: Wasn't there a woman in the play?

ROBERTA: Now it looks like there wasn't.

BILL: Okay. Put one in. That's always a good idea, and besides, I'd like to see you perform.

That afternoon they did not perform. Roberta's shoulder hurt where Magoo had dug into it, and a lingering scent of Magoo made her want to know more of him. But Agustín had thrown her out of her own house, from her own stage. That's how Roberta felt, though it wasn't exactly how it happened. He was the one who had insisted on leaving, going home, back to his horror, and she had insisted on preventing it, with shouts and quarreling and Agustín pushing his need to be alone—until Roberta wound up slamming the door, and turning the key twice so that he couldn't leave and do something crazy.

Roberta's first stop: Bill, out of a need for refuge rather than passion. Her second stop, valiantly and somewhat imprudently: Magoo's apartment, with the intention of controlling what was controllable. She still had the keys in her handbag. A neighbor saw her enter but seemed indifferent. Just to make sure, Roberta explained that she was coming to water her cousin's plants, he was away. Magoo had no plants; the neighbor shut the door in her face without listening. Rain had gotten into the apartment, and the carpeting under the window was wet. A cat, judging from the odor, had also entered through the fire escape. Otherwise no change, not even last Sunday's newspaper at the front door. Someone had stolen it. All the better. Nearly two weeks had elapsed since the event, and it was as if nothing had happened. She tried to dry the carpet, shut the window, leaving a crack open to reduce the stench of cat piss—a thousand times preferable to the odor of revolt and fear that she had smelled on her last visit.

There was little mail in Agustín's mailbox. A few brochures, a picture postcard of the obelisk from a friend in B.A., a letter from the bank, the telephone bill.

Roberta searched for Agustín's checkbook and ID in an attempt to restore him to life. As if life meant paying bills, when the greatest bill could never be settled. What bullshit.

She went to the study and slowly began organizing things on the desk. A fit of orderliness seized her and prompted her to empty drawers, find suitcases to put Magoo's clothes into. A traveler's scant belongings, she thought. Her intention was to bring them home, but she realized in the nick of time how suspicious it would look to leave hauling a couple of suitcases. Another housebreaker in this world of thugs. She considered taking just his sheepskin coat—the treasured *gamulán* of every self-respecting Argentine—and bringing him his snow boots, for winter was approaching. But no, best to leave everything there, ready for a quick getaway. Leave all of Agustín's things in the suitcases. Not even take his briefs. He could wear her panties and her sweaters and her blue jeans and her T-shirts. She would continue passing on her most androgynous clothes, as if to purify him of his past, unburden him. She would weave for him if necessary. Learn to weave for him. Envelop him in her web?

She sat down on Agustín's cot and pictured the scene. She, like a spider, spinning round and round, till she had him ensnared. And then, suck his blood? What for? It was he who seemed to want blood, she was only trying to fathom his secret. She remembered being about eighteen and feeling the urge to break a man, see what was inside. Reach his essence. It was a need to know, and a need to reconstruct him after she knew. The egg may hurt when its shell is broken, but the value lies in the yolk, she'd said to herself back then. Elusive kiddo, she commented to herself at that point, calm and somewhat exhausted after having put things so much in order.

The kitchen clean and the refrigerator empty. The books on their shelves like another New York leftover. Mostly paperbacks, typical components of the grand discard in the piled-up annexes of city debris. Who knows how many of those books Magoo had found amid the trash, neatly stacked next to metal garbage cans, what with the hyperawareness of recycling and the possibility of someone poorer or more bookish or more voracious or crazier coming by. If she threw out Magoo's books, someone would surely pick up what he in turn had picked up from some other pile, but Roberta preferred lining them all up in the study, and didn't even dream of taking Gus his favorite books. No belongings of the blasted murderer would pollute her house. Only his human presence, and that was more than enough.

She stretched out on the bed, on the mattress with its rumpled Indian bedspread, and began musing on how many times the word "murderer" had polluted her own prose. And questioning herself on whether Magoo had killed someone in order to prove more interesting in her eyes, or to approximate one of her characters, or worse yet, to *be* one of her characters. Or to replace her prose, so as to occupy places that weren't his. Or was it she who had pushed or rather instigated him through a barely hinted-at fascination?

But to what extent should she consider herself central to the situation when Agustín merely looked at her as a life preserver? Where was the boundary? How to recognize the dividing line between the written and the lived experience?

There she was disgressing, in order to avoid the most alarming of all questions: Would a onetime killer kill twice? Maybe what she really wanted was to confront him with her body, force him to write with her own blood on her very own body.

Just then she heard a faint scratching against the front door, as if a very dainty dog were trying to enter and didn't have the nerve to scratch hard. Then she thought she noticed the door-knob turn, very slowly to begin with, first to one side and then to the other, and suddenly all her questions were erased, leaving only the reply of the aforementioned body, stiff, on the alert, and a pair of darting eyes seeking a way of escape.

If the only live part of a body is the eyes, that means there is a body and it will react in the best way possible, Roberta seemed to be saying to herself at the precise moment she leaped up and raced for refuge in Agustín's study. She shut the door silently, and luckily the key was on the inside, but she realized instantly that she'd chosen the worse solution, assuming there were others. A study without a window, just a grated vent high up. She'd gotten herself into this death trap and may have found the limit she was seeking, perhaps too late.

If they were after Magoo, they would take her away. And why not? She had been playing with the weapon of the crime. And with the criminal, to boot.

Innocence is always the great absentee. Fear is ever present. Fear making her heart race and pound so loud it was audible through the door. A drum to lure them to her lair.

She couldn't tell if they'd managed to open the apartment door and were now but a few yards away. She wasn't wondering whether it was the police, the theater company, the instigators of murders, or simply some friend looking for Agustín for reasons having nothing to do with her fear. Each, in any case, might represent danger.

Seated on the floor, for the chair in front of the desk where Agustín writes or despairs is forbidden to her, she said to herself, What a pointless, shitty death. Not thinking that she had nothing to do with that sordid plot, didn't even know the dead man's name. That didn't make her less of an accomplice.

Accessory after the fact.

Accessory after the fact, she repeated like a mantra and finally her heart quieted down so other sounds could be heard. Accessory after the fact. Not a sound entered the room. As if the apartment were empty, and the building, the street, the world. All empty.

Maybe they were on the other side of the door to Agustín's tiny study, silently lying in wait. A trap.

It was night by the time she finally broke out of that enclosure which was an enclosure within her own mind—her own death. No one was in the apartment, no one waiting outside the front door. It might have been a drunk, wobbling, confused. Or only her imagination, in which case it was unbounded, everything within her an undifferentiated continuum of fear. Starting with that utterly diffuse fear of the blank page, progressing to the fear of what gestates on that page—the knowledge that belongs to us without our being able to recognize it as ours—and extending to that terror of outer threat, which might seem more real.

At a certain unexpected moment in the long wait, Roberta, unable to stand it any longer, made a bolt for the kitchen, which was next to the front door. From there she had a commanding view of Agustín's meager space and realized that she was alone. She returned to the study and scooped up what appeared to be Agustín's manuscripts, along with his ID and other papers she'd sorted out in a more lucid time. More calmly she picked up her coat, her gloves, her scarf.

She peered down the hall—empty—double-locked the door as if for the last time, and raced down the steps, not pausing to catch her breath until she reached the street.

She realized she was still holding the keys in her hand and felt like throwing them down a sewer so as to forget this house and this panic. She couldn't do that to Agustín. Come to think of it, neither could Agustín do what he was doing to her.

Anyhow. She had to regain her composure, her so-called cool. Make sure, first of all, that she wasn't being followed, that this wasn't a snare whereby she led them straight to Agustín's door. Hard to determine in this world of people running, fleeing the cold, and she herself on a freezing corner, stiff.

She decided to go into a coffee shop and keep watch through the windows.

Someone could have followed her. Someone could be patiently waiting for her outside. Who? That guy with the trench coat and broad-brimmed hat? Too classical a getup. How about the other one going back and forth, looking in all directions? A pusher, no doubt. Nobody would be that obvious; the people after Agustín were professionals, although it wasn't clear what their profession was.

Yes, it could be that guy buying a newspaper, lingering in front of the newsstand kind of hesitantly, as if waiting for a taxi. Uh-uh, because now he was climbing into the damn taxi and vanishing in traffic. Bet it's that blonde with her face half hidden in a shawl, entering the coffee shop and sitting down at the table in front. Cut it out, enough paranoia, get on with it. On to other things.

Take a look, for example, at Magoo's novel.

She opened one of the folders on the table and suddenly found herself immersed in a welter of crossings-out and erasures. Page after page. Corrected corrections again crossed out. A constant erasing and starting again over previous traces. Mere markings. Few legible words. She couldn't bear it. She opened the other folder, fastened with rubber bands, and found some notebooks. They were Magoo's journals, the detailed, methodical account of his impotence, much more unbearable than all the crossings-out and even than her feeling of being pursued.

Finish it once and for all. No matter what.

She shut the folders with a snap of the rubber bands and went in search of a phone at the rear of the coffee shop. With coin in hand she rejected the idea of calling Bill. Enough of using him as the only way out. Reserve him. Think up someone else to leave the manuscripts with. Someone neither Spanish-speaking nor curious about literature, who wouldn't try to decipher the secret before she did.

Nobody loves me. The statement suddenly, incongruously, struck her. Nobody loves me. And before letting herself wallow in self-pity she retrieved a phone number from her memory and called the least likely person, Ava Taurel. Lovely nom de guerre, she thought while dialing. Lovely, lovely, she thought, and it was an incantation for Ava to be at home and care for her just a little, enough to help her out.

"I need your help," she stated without even saying hello.

"Hi, Roberta. Whatever you want. You know my line of work is like a priesthood."

"It isn't what you imagine."

"I imagine everything, anything. My fantasy knows no limits. I'll tell you about it—I've got some sensational plans, I'm going to open a school, expand my horizons. I've put some ads in *Screw* magazine, am going to rent an office, get listed in the Yellow Pages—"

"Take it easy. Slow down. I just need you to keep some papers for me for a while, but it's urgent. I have to give them to you right away."

"I was just leaving for work. Are you far from my place?"

"Kind of."

"Then you'll have to see me in my element. They're waiting for me. Jot down the address."

Ava in fatigue gear: spike-heeled black boots, black satin corset with garter belt, net stockings, a transparent robe also black as a widow's veil. And her windblown blond mane, looking more Valkyrie than ever though never was a Valkyrie seen in such a getup.

Come in, she told Roberta, who remained standing by the front desk, facing a fat, beatific-looking receptionist. Come in, she insisted. We're having a party, I'll introduce you to everyone. You'll enjoy it. We'll leave your papers here, wherever you like—it's a mess chez moi and they can get lost there, or who knows, spattered, something like that. Just look around for a place to drop them and have some fun, meanwhile, and a couple of drinks, okay? This is Sandy, this is Roberta, a sensational writer—she'll find plenty of material here, won't she? And then I bet she'll write something about our humble little party.

The so-called Sandy smiled timidly at Roberta, lowering her eyes slightly. She was naked under a bridal gown of transparent lace, with breasts exposed and wearing a little crown of orange blossoms, and about seventy-five, to judge by her skinny flab. Her bridegroom was of the leather set: naked torso and whip at the belt.

"They're such simple souls," Ava whispered feelingly into her ear as she led Roberta through that homespun hell.

Why now? wondered Roberta while putting on an expression to greet the people Ava was introducing her to. And this one is an outstanding German dominatrix, Ava remarked, and Roberta, Hello, hello, pleased to meet you, as in the most congenial of New York cocktail parties, for it was that, too, and meanwhile on the stage a woman, with great care, with love one might almost say, was tying a fellow with long leather thongs—black, naturally—and putting a black leather hood over him and zipping it closed one orifice at a time, shutting him off from the world: the zipper over his mouth to muffle his cries, a small zipper over each eye to keep him from seeing what was about to befall him, another, slightly asphyxiating zipper over his nose. Thus, with his senses all blocked, with clamps on his nipples, he was suspended by the wrists and hoisted up in some medieval torture contraption, all wood, pulleys, wheels and ropes, which might have interested Roberta as a mechanism per se, apart from its sadistic connotation, had she not kept wondering, Why me, just on this day? Out of the frying pan into the fire.

Someone brushed past her and excused himself. A spectacled man, in leather jockstrap and metal-studded wristlets. Pardon me. He had a glass in his hand, and seemed friendly.

Each to his own disguise, muttered Roberta under her breath.

These aren't disguises, they're the real thing, said a voice. As usual.

Amid the clusters of people chatting, stem glasses in hand, clothed or partially clothed, adorned with spikes or genital rings and dog collars, some were focused on their intimate situations. One dominatrix had strapped a boy to a chair, his prick exposed and trussed like a slab of meat, the boy himself tied with one knee on the ground in an excruciating shooting stance, beaten, humiliated. Mute. These are pleasures unarticulated, unheard, even unperceived. At least unperceived by Roberta, chatting but a few steps away, trying to pose the difficult question to others: What is left to fantasy if all of one's dark desires attain reality, are acted out? There will always be a supplement, someone replied, and when Roberta turned her head, her attention was caught by a pair of deep blue eyes.

A meeting of eyes, Roberta's and the blue ones, and soon he was alongside her telling his story.

"I thought I was gay when I realized how much I liked all this, but it doesn't mean a thing, believe me, I adore women. And what I adore most is women's underwear, satin especially. I love wearing it, as you can see, but don't be fooled. I'm real macho."

No doubt about it, Roberta felt tempted to say, which accounts for your wearing a pale blue slip and pale blue bra, otherwise they would be pink.

He left no opening for ruminations, insisting, When I'm not dolled up, I spend my time fantasizing, dreaming of the moment I can put them on again, trying to hold off as long as possible, till I just can't take it anymore.

Roberta was no longer seduced by his eyes. His bland, Maidenform-colored eyes.

"And you," inquired the dainty blue creature, "having a good time here?"

"I don't think so. I can't stop thinking of all those people who are being tortured and who will be tortured absolutely against their will."

"Oh, I hadn't thought of that. Now that's an idea."

Meanwhile on stage the poor—happy—fellow was being methodically, furiously lashed with a wicker rod, each lash splitting the air, spraying blood. Why am I staying? Roberta asked herself silently, but she stayed all the same.

She also wondered whether this might not be the theater Agustín had alluded to, in which case his inexplicable crime was simply a staged scene.

After such intense fear, what is this? Fear fades away with consent, and Roberta no longer felt as if she were in a threatening world. Here threat seemed make-believe, even though blood was spurting from the guy's buttocks with every lash. That was the real danger, the unknown Russian roulette all of them were playing: contamination, being splattered by probable red death as in a very postmodernist Poe. What a bad flick, Roberta moaned to herself, what a lousy script—I'm getting out of this theater. And she was just about to leave when someone approached—another guy in a dog collar, a training collar in this case, with spikes on the inside digging into his neck at every turn, another guy ringed and spiked, handcuffed in back—who with his shoulder timidly brushed Roberta's shoulder.

"Excuse me. Ava, my mistress, wants you to come and see a certain ritual. Very enlightening, she said to tell you, and she also said to tell you that I am your slave, hers and therefore yours, and you are to do whatever you want with me. You may lead me, tied by this chain, to her feet."

"Tell your mistress I've had enough for today. Show me the way out, and here—I'm putting these folders under your arm. Take them to Ava and tell her to hide them wherever she thinks best. Please."

"Please? You said please to me? You'd better just go. This slave will carry out your orders, anyway."

"**D**o you realize what time it is? You've left me locked up, what do you want, a prisoner? You have one, without having to turn the key. I'm in your hands—nearly out of my mind. Where were you?"

"Nobody worries about me," Roberta started yelling. "And I have to worry about everyone." Nobody, nobody, wept Roberta, and she broke down in hiccups. A desperate sobbing that had been accumulating over months, years. Ever since she'd met Agustín or maybe even long before that, over a slow course of uprooting. What am I doing in this city? she was trying to articulate, stretched on her bed facedown, head between her arms. Nobody here cares about me, everyone pursues, abuses, accuses me.

Agustín, both numb and indignant, let her go on. His role was being usurped, his breath stifled, his lines recited, the sympathy due him denied, his moment upstaged. Roberta wasn't even aware of this. After crying a long while without restraint, emptying herself, she had fallen asleep with her face buried in the pillow.

Suddenly Agustín felt empty too, and finally tore himself away from the sofa, where he had intended to spend the night. He climbed into bed next to Roberta, in the small space near the wall, which he hated, and hugged her tight. We're a shipwrecked pair, he murmured in her ear, but she didn't hear him and couldn't object that it was he who was shipwrecked, she but a shipwreck's stowaway.

"I want love," was the first thing Roberta said when she awoke, her eyes swollen and the pillow still damp.

"You're asking for something I can't give you."

"I'm not talking about physical love."

"I can't give you the other kind either."

"I'm not asking it of you, I'm not making any demands on you. I want there to be love, I want to feel love and I want to be able to express it. In all directions."

"What love are you talking about? What kind of love can there be when there is killing?"

"There are those who kill for love. Forget it."

What to do with this new sense of living at a distance from oneself? What tonality to give, she wonders, to what is extracted, extraneously, from the folds of one's own sheets, in a clammy speleology of memories?

There are long patios with flowerpots, there's a large—empty?—birdcage. There are twilights and permutations. Glances. If only she could use the patios to block off other realms clamoring not to be seen. A deafening clamor.

It has to do with a latent desire to be present elsewhere, not wanting to know about that elsewhere.

Roberta.

Roberta listens to herself, and occasionally tries to write in search of herself, forgetting it's in writing that one is most apt to get lost.

Magoo flatly refuses to leave the house—*her* house—and gradually she too finds herself ensnared in that fluffy ball of yarn, that despicable cocoon of security. Agustín is no longer himself, he's another person, ascetic, with long hair and the skin of a murderer. Sometimes Roberta caresses him and he lets her, sometimes.

The days go by, a month or more; it may be snowing outside.

The checks from Agustín's grant are sent directly to the bank, and Roberta administers the account by mail. They have enough postage stamps to last them the rest of their lives. The only thing keeping them from being completely detached from the world is the walk to the incinerator, down the long hall, past the mail chute connecting all the floors. The phone is on ringer-off, the answering machine is connected at times, and some incoming messages are received but never returned. What else? Oh yes: only one of the numerous doormen began worrying about her and came upstairs to see if she needed anything. No, Roberta told him, thank you, this is an art project, you see. Living art. I plan to stay shut in the house until all the cubbies of my inner emptiness are filled. Then I'll show the result at the New Museum, she explained to the doorman at length, for she knew this might be her only chance to have some fun. And she gave him her remaining cash. The man brought a superabundance of stamps, happy to be part of artwork in progress.

Agustín was not even mentioned, Agustín presumably is not there, and occasionally this doorman—not the others—makes some friendly remark on the intercom when announcing that a food delivery is on its way up.

They phone for take-out food from the great variety of ethnic restaurants in the area, and at one point, early on, Roberta made love to Bill over the phone while Agustín was in the bathroom. But not now. Now she can't stand the notion of another world just eight floors below.

Magoo spends lengthy periods in the bathroom, visiting himself. Bereft of his beard, bereft of his clothes, bereft of his name, he ceased knowing himself when he pressed the trigger. He's even bereft of his love for Roberta, if ever he did love her, if Roberta loved him. All he has left is a hatred that was absolutely not there when he pulled the trigger.

Bitch, bitch, he says to the mirror, and thinks of how biting an insult can be in English. He isn't thinking about whom it's directed at, simply repeats the word. Bitch. Roberta? The other woman, the one who somehow got him into this, the unmentionable woman? Bitch. Facing the mirror. And involuntarily he realizes suddenly that he is simply insulting himself, for having allowed himself to reach this uncentered point.

He, who had always revered the forms of pure geometry, the crystal-clear beauty of mathematics. That's how he had written and how he had lived his life: combing his beard, carefully adjusting the knot on his tie back in the days when he wore a tie.

He emerged from the bathroom with tears in his eyes, and Roberta on her way there detected something and opened her arms to him. He crumbled in her embrace, sobbing.

Damn it, cry! It'll do you good, Roberta said. Fortunately in a low, almost inaudible voice, sparing him platitudes and allowing him to weep with his own tears.

"If each tear were a word," uttered Agustín when he could speak again, "if each tear were a word, I'd have a fat novel written by now."

"Pathetic. Tears don't imprint, they erase. Didn't you realize that? Sometimes they even erase guilt."

"You're ranting. Guilt is never erased, even if you're innocent. Just imagine when you're guilty."

"Imagining is all I do—day and night, asleep and awake. What else do you expect me to do, the two of us locked up here? I've lost track of time."

"Not me."

He pulled the bed away, and there on the wall were two rows of crossed-out strokes, each vertical day canceled in turn with a diagonal line. Not one uncrossed-out stroke, no fresh days to come: the sentence was endless.

"Where did you learn these convicts' tricks?"

"It doesn't matter. I've got a pencil hidden away. If you want, I'll loan it to you."

"All this time lost, Magoo, gone, like our sense of humor."

"For what it's worth."

"It's worth the fun. We lost laughter, everything. We've been together for God knows how many little vertical strokes and we hardly talk. We haven't even got any dialogue left, Magoo."

"Maybe we never had it," said Magoo, mounting the stationary bicycle and beginning to pedal.

"We were going to write a play, we were trying to explore, and now nothing. Stop that, will you, and let's talk a bit."

"There's nothing to be gained by talking," panted Agustín, agitated, pedaling with greater frenzy. "Go back to your writing and let me exercise. It's the only thing that does me any good," he puffed. "I'm up to thirty kilometers an hour."

"Cut it out. Let's talk."

"Thirty-three kilometers. Talk to me, look at me—demands. *Basta.*"

"Come back, Magoo, come back. Don't try to run away, it won't get you anywhere."

"It will, and don't shout!" shouted Agustín as if from a distance, sweating, crouched over the handlebar of the stationary cycle, spinning the pedals harder.

"Okay. You're giving me an idea for a story. The protagonist will be called Yolanda."

"I'm the protagonist," Agustín protested, slackening his speed.

"You're the antagonist, the agonist. Stop bugging me. Come back. Ride your vehicle back, but stop bugging me."

"Meaning I've bugged you enough."

"Meaning that this *mens sana in corpore idem* may be all the *sano* you want, but there's no splitting the two. I'm fed up with your trying to separate things. I want out, too."

"I'll loan you the bike. But make sure to chain it when you get down. They might steal it."

"Did you ever dream of being locked up with a woman and swallowing the key?"

"Yes. It's a nightmare."

"Where are we going today?"

"To Pakistan."

"We went to India yesterday. They're too much alike."

"Are we into time measurements now? What is yesterday, today, tomorrow, in this long night engulfing us? The world is ours: let's go to Japan, to Cuba, to Mexico. Let's go to Java or to Thailand."

"How about Argentina?"

"Gives me heartburn. I'd rather return to the Punjab. There's still some lamb khurma in the fridge—let's go."

"Pedaling again."

"Have to work off the world. Undigestible food."

"You want to escape."

"Great idea. Of course I want to escape, and I want to be prepared when the moment comes."

"*Corpore sano.*"

"Hey, not that again. Once upon a time there was a cement factory hidden away in the hills, in a country in the south whose name I do not care to mention. Political prisoners worked there as slaves, and cement dust destroyed their lungs. At the entrance to the plant was a sign: *"Mens sana in corpore sano."* And a prisoner was permanently stationed near the sign to remove the dust that collected on it every fifteen minutes."

"Do you know this firsthand?"

"Yes. I read it in a novel."

"I know I can leave whenever I want to. Yet I feel locked in, Rob, as if we were never going to go outside again."

"There's not much coming in either, I guess you could say. Sorry about that."

"But I am inside already. Utterly, deeply, unbearably, irremissibly inside. I feel all stopped up. I don't want to leave, or can't."

"Are you always going to switch channels when the news goes on?"

"Naturally."

"We stepped out of the world, Magoo."

"We are."

"Are we not, above all, writers? Isn't the writer a witness? I at least want to know what's happening in our country."

"Your country, you mean. I no longer have a country."

"I don't think I can stand up anymore, I'm exhausted."

"Come, babe, I'll give you a bike ride."

"No. Talk to me instead."

"Get dressed then. And bundle up 'cause we're going out and it's snowing, I think."

"Where are we going?"

"On the balcony."

"Epigrammatic, we two. No communication."

"Communication doesn't exist. It's dead—I killed it."

"Do you remember our play, the unborn one?"

"Don't talk to me."

"Do you remember love?"

"Don't talk to me."

"Do you remember me?"

"All I can think about is what I can't remember at all: the moment of the shot."

"Stand up, please, stand up. What are you doing stretched out on the rug naked, like a dead woman. You scare me."

"I'm sunbathing on a Caribbean beach, under coconut palms. You can hear the sound of the sea, and that's all I hear. There's so much silence here. The sand is warm—come enjoy the sun with me."

"No. Get up. Let's do some exercise."

"I'm busy. On the verge of understanding what writing with the body is all about."

"Writing what?"

"I don't know. My body should tell me. No, it doesn't have to tell me anything. I am my body. What I am finally going to be able to do is to put it into words, I think. Let me pay attention."

"Feminine crap. The body must be subdued, disciplined."

"Look who's talking."

. . .

"One, two, one two, onetwo."

"I can't stand seeing you on the rug anymore. If you get up, I'll tell you a story:

"A wealthy man lives over the Museum of Modern Art. One day he finds—knows he's going to find—a ticket for the museum checkroom in his mailbox. He goes to the checkroom and in exchange for the ticket is given a briefcase. In the outer pocket of the briefcase is a note that says, 'Come to the bathroom and follow instructions.' The man leaves the bathroom wearing women's underwear, buys a ticket to enter, sits down in front of the Pollocks, crosses his legs and reveals women's mesh stockings. They're hooked I think to a garter belt and he's wearing a bra, but you can't see them. Someone sits down behind him. A voice says, Now go home, lie down in bed, and put on the hood inside the briefcase. She will come upstairs but you mustn't see her; she will come upstairs and give you what's coming to you, what's coming to you."

"This is Ava Taurel stuff! Where did you come up with this?"

"From your answering machine, love. I don't like your friends and I like their messages even less, and hoods much, much less. I detest hoods. They bring back bad memories."

"You can leave whenever you want, Magoo."

"Are you throwing me out?"

"You turn everything around, distort it. Now you're going to make me believe that I was the one who locked you in, when I'm the one who's locked in. Because of you."

"No one is holding you back. You can go out whenever you want."

"I don't go out because I'm afraid, how about you? Or do you think I don't believe we're being watched with spyglasses? Do you think I have the blinds drawn because I'm bothered by the squalid winter light?"

"I didn't mean to do it. I'm not to blame for having killed her."

"What?"

I'm not to blame for having—"

"You told me it was a man."

"That's what I said. I lied. I don't know why I lied. Anyhow, it's all the same. I think I didn't want to make you jealous, I didn't want to complicate everything, as if everything weren't already hopelessly complicated. It's all the same, don't you see? We were talking about Vic when we could still talk about it. And besides, a man wouldn't be preparing soup. I thought you would have picked up on that."

No. Roberta hadn't picked up on that, the thought hadn't occurred to her. Suddenly she needed time to think, and space especially, she needed space. Her first reaction was to want to kick Agustín out of the house. Fling his belongings after him and bolt the door

but: not a single one of Agustín's belongings was around

but: she was already too involved in this mess to solve it by throwing him out

but: she had no strength left

She began to feel cold, went into her walk-in closet to get a shawl or something, pulled the light cord, noticed the vast disorder, pulled the cord again, shut the door, and in the darkness made herself a nest of sweaters and turtlenecks, slacks, blankets, shawls, and an old fur jacket that were all scattered on the floor.

Like in Bill's shop, she mused. Why didn't it occur to me sooner? And she fell asleep.

Agustín has improvised a pair of dumbbells from some bronze paperweights. Stretched out on the rug he seems to be working his triceps. Then he turns over and begins doing push-ups. In Mexico they call them lizards, he says to himself, as if exercise and the words defining it are the only things that exist for him.

A man who gripped a revolver
cut himself off from himself
doesn't seem to notice Roberta's absence
doesn't think about his own lie
murderer and liar—too heavy, better the paperweights.
one, two, up, down. Inhale, exhale.
breathing is what counts, the breath of life goddammit
love is what matters to Roberta
precisely for that reason she doesn't even mention it anymore,
what is love, I wonder?
to kill for love?
for displaced love?
But then the bullet would have struck the heart, not the temple. It was as if he'd wanted to send her ideas flying. To shatter thought.

I'm the one who wants to stop thinking and can't. I cannot. One, two. Up, down. Working out, as they say here. Working toward the outside, from the outside, on the outside? That is, giving it your all, as if sweat were thought.

Roberta has buried herself in the closet. I wish her name were Constance, she deserves it.

I said man to her, not woman. And shaved off my beard outer signs, all of them

there are others in the innermost recesses, undecipherable signs.

Will Constance come out, be born for me, or will she always be a wedge in this house, one more wedge in my conscience?

Constance, come out of your double enclosure. Roberta, Bobbie, Bob. Forgive me. I need forgiveness, I need to forgive myself and I can't.

Exercise as punishment. Like forced labor. Prisoners, the cement factory, prisoners, *desaparecidos*, forced laborers. Like a galley slave, to expiate guilt. To reduce it, locked in this galley of my body without allowing myself even a breather, only the breathing in and out of the exercise to help in this rowing motion that pulls me far from myself, farther and farther from myself and my contrition.

Roberta, inside the closet, is lost in her night terrors. The same ones that used to awaken her in childhood, at times leaving her glued to the sheets, and at times impelling her to wander through the long corridors of the dark house, a reckless feat, to make sure the front door was locked. She so little she barely reached the latch.

Now at least she knows that the fears of these last nights with Agustín don't stem from any external threat or even from the undismissed possibility of his having another fit. Assuming that there actually was a fit, that the crime really happened and wasn't another one of Agustín's lies. So it was a woman, not a man. What did Agustín have in mind in the initial telling?

Someone planted a seed of terror in her. Or else it's her own seed and it has grown. In which case, if her fear doesn't stem from outside, she says to herself, she can tell herself This is me: my fear. My fear is part of me and there's nothing to be frightened of. Agustín. Agustín, this fear that's part of oneself is the worst of fears, wanting to suppress it can make you kill.

It was daytime when Roberta emerged from her lair and she needed to see light outside. For the first time after being in the dark so long she raised the blinds. The reflection of snow filled the highly charged room. External ghosts no longer frightened her; she was certain now that all the terror was contained right there.

Magoo was on the bed, asleep, facedown, head resting on his arm, sweat virtually dry, still sheathed in Roberta's jogging suit. He looked more like remains than a sleeping person—cast up by the tide onto this beach where he remained, without leaving a trace on the sand, without getting under the covers.

"Magoo," Roberta called when the coffee was ready. "I mean, Agustín, Agustín Palant, it's time we touched land."

PART

Let's go outside now, slowly. Come, we're getting there, one foot after the other, carefully, as if we had no choice, as if the only way to go were forward. That's it. I'll take your hand and we'll keep going.

(My hand? I don't want to be taken by the hand, I hate to be led. It makes me furious. I'm not a blind man, I know my way, I think. No, I don't. I have no way. No one can show me what I don't have.)

Close your eyes. Let's keep going. Come. Carefully, easy does it. Let's go, Gus, speed it up, but don't step on the peddlers' wares. That's it. Be careful on the ice, don't step on the rags, the pants and shoes and old dresses displayed on the sidewalk, don't step on the old magazines spread out for sale like carpets so many people must have stepped on and will keep stepping on.

(I don't step, I levitate. I never want to set foot on these streets again. I refuse to talk, won't open my mouth.)

Come on, we're doing fine. Don't worry about the cars, I'll guide you. Don't open your eyes. Now we're in front of the big black cube, remember? The huge iron cube perched on an angle. They call it a sculpture. Some guys are trying to make it turn, they are laughing. Open your ears but not your eyes. Never your eyes. There are some white circles painted on the cube, like dice. Gigantic dice.

(*Un coup de dé.*)

Get moving, Gus. I know, you're thinking about the role of

chance. That will get you nowhere. Don't stop, don't think. We'll soon be there, then we'll know where, to quote our illustrious gaucho.

(As though moving were easy. I don't want a foot of mine getting ahead of my body and betraying me. No more betrayals from my body.)

We have to cross, Gus. Cross one street and then another and another. I'll guide you. There's that horrible, menacing subway entrance, that toothless, green-tongued witch's mouth, but no, they've changed it. If you opened your eyes—but don't—you'd see how different it is. It's like a gazebo now with a vaulted roof, sort of like the big greenhouse in our old botanical garden, remember? Didn't you used to go to the gardens back home, to stroll along paths swarming with cats amid labeled plants? Remember the main hothouse, that green metal structure as French as an Impressionist painting? How many times must we have crossed paths and sat on the same bench without recognizing each other! And now, so close yet so far, here we are passing by the new structure over the subway entrance which restores it to its original form of the twenties, as the sign indicates, but don't turn around or open your eyes, restores it to its origin and sets us inside a time machine, a space and language machine of memory, of those things that will never be restored to us.

(I don't have to listen to her. Wish she'd stop gabbing, enough to be following her, playing this idiotic game of blindman's buff with her as if my eyes were blindfolded, as if I were abducted, covered with a hood like so many others in my country. I don't want to be one of them, don't want to see them, never wanted to, back in my own country, and don't want to be like them now. No reason for me to get into this game.)

This wasn't here before either. Astonishing. I think you'll just have to open your eyes, everything's been changed on us. This neighborhood is different, it won't scare you anymore. No more. What was here before, where this postmodernist bar is now? What was on this corner and the other one? How long ago was before? Were we shut in for that long? There's an art gallery here now, imagine that, in this neighborhood, no less. And another gallery and another. It's like in a dream. Just hold on to my shoulder, we're almost at Tompkins Square. I bet the park hasn't changed much. The same trees, oaks, squirrels, terror lurking in the shadows. The park will give us a point of reference. This street seems much busier than before. No more sinister glances, barely a flitting shape or shadow. It's as if light has been let in, or something, and it's not on account of the cold but some other intangible. There are more shops, more brightly lit, the dealers seem to have been swept away, the streets have a smiling air, can you imagine it? This is the Lower East side, Loísa, the Bowery, the pits—the last place you'd imagine smiles.

"C'mon, stop it. Have we reached the park yet?"

"Wow! You spoke! I thought the thinking machine got your tongue. The way the cat got our tongue when we were kids, as they used to say. I hear your thinking machine going crack, crack with its badly oiled gears, going crunch, crunch, eating up your neurons. Like when we used to make love, ages ago, remember? I'd hear your thinking machine in full blast just when it should have been nice and quiet in its corner like still water. That machine doesn't let you live."

"Death is what doesn't let me live. And your chatter. Do me an enormous favor and shut up."

"But I'm still your guide, we're still in the game."

"What a game! I'm opening my eyes now, I'm talking. So as not to hear my own crunching, if you like. Goddammit. Where have you taken me? And why? Again."

"No, not again. Isn't this another path even if it's the same one? Open your eyes wide, take a good look. It sounds like a cheap metaphor but it's sheer reality—take a good look, I say. Are these by any chance the ominous quarters you once penetrated? That required the backup of a revolver? Come on! All the punks in town sport their spiky crests here, as if they were at home."

"Cut it out. It's not my fault if these boondocks have been transformed on me, if the libretto has been changed."

"Cheer up. What changed is the scenery. The site of your famous encounter is now so different, so completely washed and gentrified, it's as if the encounter hadn't taken place. Because the place no longer exists, it's different, and as we very well know, space and time are the same thing and therefore the time of the encounter, and so on."

"Nothing is erased."

"But everything is transformed."

"Us."

"Yes. We're totally changed. All we have to do now is paint our hair green, to blend into the picture. Look around you. What used to be terrifying outside is now shown in art galleries. Look, everything now is food for an exhibition. It's fantastic. I wonder what happened. And when did it happen? How long did we stay inside?"

"How long?"

"Don't throw me off. Quit jiggling me, Gus. How should I know? A month, two months, I don't know. It felt like years."

"House arrest."

"Could be. Consider yourself now cleansed of guilt."

"If only one could be cleaned like at the dry cleaner's."

"If only one could recover just a touch of joy. If we could go back to before. Let's sit down again on the park bench."

"As if time hadn't passed—"

"—more than it should have."

"As if that kind of stage were still in front of us, all covered with graffiti, turned into a garbage dump."

"As if now, all painted and dolled up, it hadn't been converted into what would be called in our dear country to the south an acoustical conch. Right? An acoustical conch, imagine. Let's go home, Agustín, to our home home, our motherland, to the acoustical conch."

"It wouldn't be such a bad idea if you shut up. Take a look—some masked creatures are climbing your famous acoustical conch. All we need now is a play. Look, maybe they're Pantalone and Harlequin. Let's go. I'm cold."

No one else would dream of brushing the snow off a park bench and sitting. Only us.

After being shut in for so long.

No.

Only us. And that other character over there, who's barefoot.

Brother chimney sweep, tightrope walker. Roberta has seen him many times, pedaling in the other park, perched on his unicycle, dressed all in black with a tattered black top hat, she's seen him come and stretch his rope between two trees, at any height. Height is inconsequential, all he cares about is walking in air upon that tautness that is like a sigh.

But she'd never seen him venture so far east of paradise before, at the very sinister edge. Destitute black smudge against the indecent whiteness of the snow.

"Let's go and warm up in your black friend's shop, let's plunge in the rags."

"What shop are you talking about? It's probably not there anymore, this neighborhood has changed. Hard-core pushers used to have a field day here in the park, and now no one's even offered us a joint. What are you talking about? Everything looks freshly scrubbed here, and Bill's shop had a different look. If we go there now, we'll surely find an impeccable Japanese restaurant, or a chic mini discotheque. Let's change neighborhoods, and strategy. If we couldn't find your theater earlier, it's unlikely we'll find it now."

"I wonder."

"Wonder on your own. Don't ask me to open my mouth again—my pipes are frozen."

"Did you see them? They're eating each other up, one literally disappearing into the arms of the other."

"They're embracing."

"No, they're devouring each other, I assure you."

"It's a performance, Roberta, can't you see there are people watching them?"

"They love each other."

"Don't talk nonsense. Let's go back to your place."

"I'm not going back, not going back, not going back, I'm never going back there. Never. I never want to see those walls again."

"We're going to freeze, Rob. Let's go. I wonder—"

"Off we go."

"I want more soup—it's not really soup but it's hot. Gus, be nice, ask for some more."

"Enough. We're already too conspicuous. What a dive you've picked! A place you want to escape from, not go into. It isn't even safe to walk past the entrance; you have to cross the street when you go by, to avoid all these bums, these hoodlums, derelicts, addicts."

"Don't talk so loud."

"Filthy, shitty place. Look how they're staring at us. Let's split. We're giving ourselves away, just look at how they're dressed. Let's go home."

"Can't go back, just have some soup. Soup. No one's going to squeal on us. This is the Salvation Army, and a salvation army saves, it doesn't condemn or denounce. We need it."

"An army's an army."

They are huddled in a corner of the enormous, virtually bare room. Far from the radiators even, as far as possible from the ragged souls who in fact have noticed the presence of these two utterly different intruders, wearing shoes that aren't lined with newspapers and only one overcoat apiece—totally unlike the bundles of clothes. So conspicuous, those two in a far corner of this no-man's-land where no one appears to be looking at them. They seem to have ceased to exist, stiff, as they grip their empty bowls, ever so still while the bundles of clothing tremble and scratch and whine.

. . .

"Scratch my back, be a good girl."

"I can't. My hands are numb, my heart is numb, and to touch someone you need a spark of human warmth, even the minutest speck of a spark of warmth. I'm wiped out."

"I wonder what we're doing in this corner on this long wooden bench against this long wooden table covered with spit and vomit, a mighty stench all around and us with no sense of smell, bathed in the odor of nothingness that surrounds us like an aura."

"The smell of gunpowder."

"I wonder."

Roberta doesn't want to be open to questions. No longer wants to or maybe never did, really. Just to remain where she is, enveloped in herself as she was enveloped in the clothes in her closet, or rather, enveloped like the others in tattered bundles taken from trash cans, sweater over sweater over filthy shirts over jackets and rags, a protective layer of clothes as in Bill's shop, romping with Bill, but that was in another life, another time, another clime, other latitudes of the soul that perhaps can never be revisited, returned to. One never goes back, never. She can just remain here like a newcomer, she who always felt like a bag lady, the bags made of writing paper. What a joke! Mere graphics, a fantasy or dream or nightmare of being a bag lady deep down, carrying all her worldly possessions in paper bags, sitting on a park bench expecting anything except a question.

And Agustín is asking questions. I wonder, he repeats like a refrain.

Roberta knows very clearly that he's incapable of providing his own answer, that the answer he's waiting for, if indeed he is, must come from her, that Agustín's self-questioning is directed at her.

And she's doing just fine without self-questioning. Fine amid all the alien clothing that exudes human warmth accumulated over centuries. She sits there with no sensation in her feet and before that none in her hands and barely any in her head, and it is so good.

Good, she says aloud, and Agustín takes that as a signal to leave. Yes, let's go, he says; this is wild.

No, it's good, this is good. I don't want to leave.

You're crazy, he says in a low, low voice so that the others don't take it personally.

Roberta, without looking at him, slides down along the wall onto the floor, and remains huddled up waiting to regain possession of her feet. It's very cold. Even if my feet come back, she says to herself, I'm not walking anymore. This is as far as I go.

Agustín slides down beside her, an act of mimicry, of being as inconspicuous as possible under this gloomy, pitiless light.

"I'm wondering what makes you go along with me, what leads you to help in my search."

"I don't know, don't ask. Or yes, I do know. It must have something to do with my childhood. A story: I too am looking for the end of a story."

"*Basta*, please. When are we going to touch land, the so-called reality?"

"Here and now. At this precise moment in this very real place."

"I'm not referring—"

"Of course not—"

"There was a story, you were saying—"

"Yes, it was being read to me so that I'd eat. At the age of five, imagine. A horror story, that's how I learned about encephalic matter. Encephalic matter? I asked. Yes, they answered, the brains. It was a dreadful, stormy night, and the two chaps in the story took refuge in an abandoned house in the middle of the forest. Just picture the scene. Thunder and lightning bolts, stuff like that. When I asked what bolts were, they gave me this unbelievable description of flames creeping under your door and chasing you, so I also became terrified of lightning. But that was later on. That day it was mostly encephalic matter. That is, those two chaps taking refuge on the ground floor of the abandoned house, hearing noises and creaking sounds, panic-stricken but trying to calm each other by saying it's the wind. No. It isn't the wind. It's the murdered woman pacing the top floor with an ax in her hand. Her encephalic matter is exposed; someone killed her by hitting her on the head with the ax, and she's seeking revenge. Sorry, I shouldn't have told you this. Anyhow, I don't know how the story ends. My mother came in just then and said, Do you think that's a story for a child? and well, they stopped reading to me, but that night I kept screaming and hallucinating, seeing doors and windows opening up, and the woman, all that. I never found out how that story ended, and now who knows how any story does."

"You're always downgrading me to the level of fiction."

"Shut up and go to sleep, we're safe here. I'm not going back home at night and don't know whether I'm ever going back."

Hours later she was awakened by a woman's shrieks and noticed that Agustín was no longer beside her. She felt a kind of relief to be alone in this very alien, hazy, unreal world of Flemish painting, a court of miracles where she could voluntarily plunge into other lost, alien, shadowy, disconcerting worlds. Via memory she could return to places inaccessible to her pen, the trip along the Yugoslavian coast, for example, and the real-life story of the aged child.

Not writing it but recalling it once again as though recounting it to Agustín—but where had Agustín vanished? She was beginning to get scared when a toothless old woman told her they always took the men to another room to sleep. Yep, there's still some decency left in this world the old woman informed her, while the other woman kept screeching.

That little boy on the boat trip was beautiful. They were going from Rieka to Split, a languorous evening of sailing with people singing on deck. The little blond boy in wooden clogs scampered about freely on the deck, happy. Maybe Roberta would have liked to have a child like that, with those same clogs and the skill to get around in them, going here and there, climbing the ladders on the boat, being part of the deck and the laughter. The boy's young mother seemed to pay little attention to him. She was with a swarthy young man and it looked like a love newly begun. Night descended, the singing gradually faded, becoming more intimate, the little boy fell asleep on his mother's lap and the mother covered him lovingly with her jacket and shielded his feet in their tiny clogs so that no one would step on them, while with her free hand she caressed the young man alongside her, and love blossomed with the night. Roberta felt cold on deck. She decided to go sleep in the ship's dining room, where many passengers already occupied the long banquettes next to the tables. At dawn she was awakened by the sounds of arrival. Still half asleep, she sat up in her seat and, at the rear of the room, caught sight of the young woman sitting at a table with her lover of the night before. Already they were quarreling. You could tell from their head movements that they were arguing, from the way their stiffened shoulders moved apart. Luckily, Roberta said to herself, the sweet child is sleeping, unaware of the fight. His little wooden clogs stuck out at the edge of the banquette on the other side of the table. Suddenly the mother's lover stood up and vanished. Arrival was imminent. Then the clogs abandoned the horizontal, may have tried to touch the floor, remained suspended in midair, and the head that appeared wasn't that of the sweet little boy but of a man who was also blond, with curly hair, indeterminately old, stooped—and Roberta, amid the somnolence of an arrival at dawn at an unknown city and the resonance of a language so strange and incomprehensible, thought she understood the magic of love which within even a minuscule span encompasses an entire life. A night on a boat can also encompass a life, and the little boy of last night had grown old because right next to him love had been born, had blossomed, and waned.

And now, demanded Roberta once again, where is love in this strange boatlike realm of human misery, where, in this blind navigation of mine, adrift on a ship of fools?

The toothless old woman dragged herself over to Roberta to console her.

They'll soon be returning your man to you, just wait and see, they always return everything. That's the worst. Not being able to get rid of anything, that's the worst. See? I have three hats when I can get along with two, one for each ear, but no, I wanted to leave one behind on a fence and somebody ran after me and said, Lady, lady—imagine calling me a lady!—you forgot your lovely hat. A wise guy. What lovely hat was he talking about? It was just an old cap as moth-eaten as me that I wore on top of the other ones, but it was warm outside and I wanted to get rid of it but it was returned to me because it was really mine. What's really yours is always returned. Now the cap helps me hold on to my dreams and even my nightmares, and I like it when the men are taken out and we're left alone to dream and have nightmares without them seeing us, but wait and see, your man will be returned, don't be afraid.

Roberta barely had time to think that that was precisely what she was afraid of, that the man would be returned; she couldn't think because another old woman, not as old and more realistic, addressed her.

Take advantage and snooze a little more 'cause we don't have much time before the men get back from the shelter and there are bathrooms if you want to go but I don't recommend them much and the worst of it is that if you go in to take a shit and they catch you, they'll want you to take a bath—what for?—and lucky it's not hot outside or they'd come in with hoses, they're poison, the street's better, the street is a thousand times better, but the other day MaryJo froze to death and we don't want to wind up like old MaryJo though she knew how to bundle up and protect herself and always found a bottle with some leftover beer in the trash baskets in the park—she could smell beer from far away but it didn't prevent her from freezing to death the other night the poor thing and they told us about it so that we wouldn't leave, but if you really have to, you can go to the bathroom, and if you hang around, they'll soon come with some hot liquid they call tea and some bread and after that you have to leave 'cause they don't let you stay here, so you better sleep now all you can 'cause it's cold outside and the doorways are freezing even though they're much more alluring.

Sleep, sleep, the old woman kept insisting, as if it were simply a matter of heeding her advice, while the screamer began screaming again, in a shriller tone because the day was breaking.

Roberta closed her eyes to please those mothers who seemed to have cropped out of the earth, from the deepest sewers, dwellings of blind alligators. She knew about those sewers, the secret tunnels where many a destitute takes shelter in winter. She also knew about the blind alligators, denizens of darkness and miasma. And all the rest. She had chanced to attend a play in the most dismal alley of the city, had gotten her shoes smeared with dog or maybe human shit to watch them perform in their burlap costumes among the veils of tattered night. That was at the end of summer, in another century so to speak. Roberta had sat on the benches improvised from boards and boxes, next to the drunks and junkies who hung around, and had watched the play about rats and sewers and dead people dealing with terror and blind alligators.

Back-alley premonitions, that's all, for who sent her after a bright party to go against the current and stick her nose in an utterly bizarre scene—but not really that bizarre in this city awash in the waters of astonishment. That is what she always loved about the city, the possibility of turning a corner and finding a totally unforeseen, inconceivable world. In the world of tomorrow all yesterdays merge in lament; at the navel of the world all the wondrous things, and all the fuzz can collect. She can see that first scene now as if in replay: a woman in a long dress, swathed in black veils, advances down the alley toward an eerie light. She looks like just another pedestrian at first, the reverse side of the boisterous party, decorated with flowers and balloons, Roberta has just attended, but the woman isn't walking aimlessly, she has a mission and is heading toward certain voices. And in the background, perched at a window, hanging from the bars, illumined by strong flashlights, another woman is howling. It is theater, once again or perhaps for the first time, theater raising a nonexistent curtain. The black-veiled woman may be death advancing toward the dull lights. A slit so that Roberta may begin to see the other side.

And for the hundredth time she wonders why Gus has lied to her, why this travesty of death? It was a woman, he killed a woman, not a man, and now his story sounds more plausible and more terrifying to me. Agustín, whom did you kill in that woman? Who do you think I am that I need deception? Whom can you have wanted to kill in all this?

The two old women keep crooning, Sleep, sleep, you're so young and pretty—and Roberta feels neither, nor can she sleep with all that racket. Soon they'll be bringing tea which is good for the stomach, they tell her, and the boys'll be coming back, they're not much good but help to pass the time. Roberta doesn't tell them her home is four or five blocks from there, with an assortment of tea if any is left, and Greek and Turkish and Chinese and Japanese food in the fridge, all mixed together because they were sending out by phone for days and days and days and kept combining them till it was one gummy mass, a gumbo unrecognizable to the palate, somewhat like themselves.

That's how we are, she says to herself, and adds: I'm now bonded to Agustín forever
because
he didn't aim at the heart but
at the brain and I told him the story about the encephalic matter just like that, out of sheer undefined cruelty, and he lied to me when he said his victim was a man, and in some part of the two of us dark vengeance is lurking, although now we won't know where or why or against whom.

No sooner does she open her eyes than she finds Agustín standing and gazing down at her, somewhat majestically if one overlooked certain details, the wrinkles on his face and in his clothes and the absence of a tie, unforgivable in him in light of his former appearance.

"Your beard's growing."

"Yes. Let's go."

"Wait, they're bringing us tea. I want to say goodbye—I can't leave just like that."

"Where do you think you are? It's my turn now, and I insist. Let's brush our teeth, take a shower, make a fresh start."

"You go, I'll give you the keys. I'm not going back. There's food all mixed together in the fridge. I'm not going back."

"We won't go to your place, we'll go to mine. I'll get my clothes, my things, my mail. We'll call the tenant subletting the apartment and say I just came back from a trip, she'll let us in. Then we'll see. But you are not staying here."

"I'm going to the bathroom."

"It's disgusting in there. Let's run over to your place, you can do what you have to do, and then we'll leave and not go back for a while if that's what you want. But come on, let's go, because
•my body can't take such desolation anymore and you bring me to this shelter of the lost, the naked, the insane, the walking dead,
•my body can't take such desolation anymore and you tell me that you're here with me just to find the end of a macabre story that isn't even mine,
•my body can't take such desolation anymore and you refuse to go back, to pull yourself together,
•my body can't take such desolation anymore and you talk to me about exposed brains as if I could tolerate such outrage. Such shamelessness."

"No, I can't go back home."

"•Look, my body can't take such desolation anymore and that's why I've had it with desolation. Look, the end of a story is never known, the only ending is death.
•Look, I had this nightmare of yours all night without even sleeping and that's enough of catching each other's nightmares. I mean, that stuff about encephalic matter."

"You're right. Enough is enough."

Agustín finally managed to pull Roberta away from the island of delusion and dragged her as far away as possible, to a coffee shop. Just two blocks. Stay here, he told her; order something, no problem, don't be afraid. Give me the key to your place and I'll go and get some things. Then I'll come back and we'll have a bite and I'll pay and we'll decide what to do, but meanwhile you can go to the toilet and have a nice hot cappuccino, a bite to eat, and come back to life. At least to the same life as yesterday. Remember? When we spoke as more or less rational creatures, more or less normal human beings. Just yesterday.

Roberta apparently said or murmured, A lifetime, as if an entire lifetime had elapsed since the previous day, and Agustín, in turn, realized that he'd failed to specify what he was going to look for but assumed—wrongly—that she must have assumed he was going to get money or a credit card or at least the card for the money machine, or anything else for paying; even a check.

That at least was his intention when he entered Roberta's apartment. All he had to do was look in the top bureau drawer, where he was sure to find something of the sort. But no, he didn't go to the bureau drawer. He felt the need to investigate other crannies, and searched the bed, underneath the mattress, in the space between wall and bed, and between mattress and mattress cover. As if he were looking for some lingering trace of their lovemaking in a fold of the blanket. Or looking for some other unmentionable item. Then he headed toward Roberta's worktable, where the papers were covered with dust. He wanted to read the manuscripts, find out what she'd been working on just before and perhaps during his eruption into her life. But what was he actually going to read if what he was looking for had never been written: the end of a macabre story. Or rather, its epiphany.

The confusion of this desk, he thought. Like Roberta's mind. Then he regretted the analogy. And regretted thinking and regretted regretting, and regretted especially thinking about the mind. That forbidden enclosure. Brains spattering everything now. The woman with the ax is looking for revenge and he knows that the woman with the ax can't get him because he

Why did you lie to me, why didn't you tell me it was a woman?

Why did you aim at the head and not the heart?

asks Roberta from the depths of every hollow of that realm abandoned by her in self-imposed exile.

A woman is pacing the top floor with an ax in her hand and her skull split in two by a bullet, no, by an ax, seeking to return blow for blow.

An eye for an eye.

She is waiting to retaliate.

Roberta told him the story without an ending, the perpetual nightmare.

Roberta's retaliation

a woman is groping behind all of us with an ax in her hand.

The executioner's ax, the spattering of brains.

Agustín enters the closet from which Roberta had emerged the previous morning, to make himself a nest perhaps. When he finds one already there, he dashes out, fleeing once more from himself

and he recalls the other thing.

But if I just wanted to take a leak. But if I just wanted to brush my teeth, or shave.

He goes into the bathroom, performs none of these pressing functions, performs

or does not. He responds again to the inner command that prompts his search. He rummages in the medicine cabinet, tosses bottles to the ground, breaks one, filling the room with medicinal smells, cuts himself, ignores it, hunts, pokes around, inspects, climbs up on the side of the bathtub and is on the verge of slipping off, of cracking his skull on the edge of the tub, as though it were an ax, regains his balance, can't help scraping away desperately, like a dog after a bone, a dog trained to detect drugs but hungering for something else.

At last he stumbles upon a hard object. He halts in his tracks. His entire being comes to a halt, everything that had been galloping inside him halts, even his blood seems to halt, and in a flash he sees his own hands in the mirror. He sees them utterly white, spectral, and on one of them that black smudge: the revolver.

So we meet again, pal.

With this barely formulated remark, stripped of emotion, he goes into the bedroom and throws himself on the bed. Then begins moving the revolver over his face, slowly, with his eyes shut. It isn't an ax. It is something rounded and smooth and cold, imperceptibly getting warm. He doesn't know or need to know that the revolver has been unloaded. Pressing it against his temple therefore is a sincere gesture. But he doesn't squeeze the trigger.

He assumes Roberta is waiting for him.

Roberta is not waiting where he assumes. Roberta hasn't even ordered a glass of water in the coffee shop but has gone back to the shelter. Everyone, despite the cold and the snow, is outside; the place is being hosed down.

"It's insulting, like they're washing us," says the three-hatted woman.

Roberta opens her mouth to make some sensible remark on the need for cleanliness, but closes it immediately, realizing that this sort of statement belongs to the other Roberta, the one who fell asleep on a bench the night before and, without awakening, has simply gone off looking for the end of a nightmare or, perhaps, for revenge, depending on one's view.

Let's go over to the little square with the benches, says the old woman with the three hats. Roberta follows her and then sits down next to her. It's pretty here, says the old woman, looking at the old church with its sharp spire. When it gets warmer the squirrels come out, you'll see them, says the old woman. Then she hands the third hat to Roberta, and Roberta accepts it, just as she accepts the idea of sitting next to this same old woman and seeing at long last, when it's warm again, squirrels in this minimal triangular haven.

Having found what he was after in the top drawer of the bureau—or having found it earlier, in the bathroom—Agustín is now descending in the elevator, on his way to Roberta. He passes his hand over his face, feels the rather heavy growth, thinks that within a few days it won't be so stubbly, it will begin being a beard like the one he had, and everything will be back on track. The revolver in his pocket is no comfort; neither does it scare him.

He walks toward the coffee shop where he left Roberta. Thinks about ordering a good breakfast for both of them, with bacon and eggs, something they're not so accustomed to eating, but this time it'll be a way of becoming part of the city, accepting its sunnier side and not continuing to thrash about in the dark. Make the eggs sunny side up.

Then he'll see.

En route he starts thinking up jokes to tell Roberta in the coffee shop, about eggs and the sun, Falangist eggs facing the sun, plus other more obvious connotations; he won't mention the revolver, will pull her out of the pit with laughter and later, when alone, tend to his private ghosts.

Roberta is not in the coffee shop and his good intentions collapse. He's frightened. Maybe the pit has already swallowed Roberta. He runs. Headed toward the shelter, naturally, toward the thing that he is unable to offer her.

And he finds her farther on, in the prowlike triangle, with uneven cobblestones and bare trees, beneath the wintry light.

The sun has faded, a mere glow on the horizon, not a trace of yolk in the light, an icy glimmer.

At first he fails to recognize Roberta, who's wearing the old woman's cap and is huddled against her.

She behaved real nice, says the old woman to Agustín when at last he holds out his hand to Roberta. She behaved real nice. As if she were referring to a dog or a child left in her care.

Roberta stands up, takes off the cap, and extends it to the old woman, who refuses to take it. About to put it on again and to resume her seat on the bench, Roberta makes an enormous effort, leaves the cap on the spot she'd previously occupied, waves goodbye to the woman, and, as she walks off alongside Agustín, says, "You know something? They have readings and lectures at the nondenominational church. I was invited once and read three stories."

And then gazes at him, startled. Scared. As if she had mentioned something unspeakable.

Agustín helped her into a cab and, once inside, embraced her, leaned her against him, kissed her hair over and over, after so many centuries, thought Roberta, after so much unlived life.

I found it, he said finally, in a whisper, in French, so as to feel utterly foreign or to keep the driver from understanding, provided of course that the driver wasn't Haitian. *Je l'ai trouvé.* What did you find, Roberta asked in Spanish. The thing you hid in the bathroom, I found it. Now we can dispose of it, both of us together, so it won't come between us.

The cab left them at the Christopher Street pier. It was almost dark and a terrible idea to be walking out there, but they had no choice. As they approached the pier, the memory of similar ceremonies that had taken place in their own country to the south, ceremonies undoubtedly filled with genuine threat, diminished Roberta's fear of present threats of another sort.

Both knew about it. On the wooden boards of this very dock there are men who allow themselves to be chained, face up or down, and stay there all night at the mercy or delight of whoever happens by. Anyone can do as he pleases with them. By morning some are floating in the river, irrevocably, facedown.

Agustín knew about the bodies floating in the river and also about the others, hurled half alive from helicopters, bellies slit open so they wouldn't float. Those of the north and those of the south. They asked for it, people would say down there. The ones truly asking for it are these guys, and still. He'd have to give more thought to these symmetries, but no, yes, anything to avoid thinking of the revolver he was carrying once again in his pocket, now wrapped in a handkerchief. He took it from his pocket openly and threw it into the dark water. Because of the cold there were no men around, either tied up or otherwise.

Only chunks

of ice

floating by.

At this point Roberta agreed to return to her apartment. Agustín cleaned the tub, they took a bath together and soon afterward, still damp, fell asleep in each other's arms.

The next morning Agustín was laughing as he put up the coffee. You finally woke me up, he said to Roberta. I didn't wake you at all, you woke up by yourself. Another kind of awakening, he tried to explain without explaining anything, just letting the incongruity go.

After that he went out and she thought he was going to pick up some bread or croissants, but he came back with flowers. This is a fresh start, he said. I've had a bellyful of tragedy. Enough melodrama.

Easy to say, Roberta was about to reply but she didn't simply because she wanted something to be finished with, to halt that slow slide toward the void.

"Can't you see, Gus, the ridiculousness of all this? If everyone eventually dies, gradually or suddenly, what difference does one more shove make? Not to mention that we never had a good look at your famous weapon—maybe it was just a deceit, a mere theater prop, a revolver for blanks, and the guy who sold it to you really ripped you off and now we've thrown it in the river and will never know, not to mention that the gun shop where you bought it has by now most likely been turned into a porno bar or something of the sort. The Weapon Cabaret, where all aim at each other and no one hits the target."

"You're right. We fall like bowling pins, we fall like flies, and here we are making desperate attempts at a few more flutters. What a gas, what a joke, what a laugh, all a great act those theater people had me play with globs of tomato sauce, because I think there was blood, yes, there was blood, and I refuse to remember any more—all this stuff here in the land of ketchup, of ersatz. And your dead woman with her brains exposed keeps wandering around on the top floor in search of revenge, not revenge for the ax blow but for the platitude of the plot they stuck her in, poor thing, just imagine, smeared forever with her own brains. What a nuisance, how tacky. Makes you want to weep."

They wept together, and once again fell asleep—always sleeping, it seems—and Roberta was awakened by her own voice answering the phone, for one of them at some point had raised the volume of the answering machine: Hello—as if nothing had happened in all that time—we're away on a trip, please leave your message.

"Come, come, come," insisted a shrill voice on the other end of the line. "This is Lara, it's absolutely essential that you come to my place Saturday night, you and your Latin lover. If the two of you are writing a play, you must get to know the group. I'm expecting you both—you *must* be back by now."

"Forget it," Roberta answered into the air. "We're not writing anything anymore."

"To the contrary," Agustín muttered much to his regret. "To the contrary, we're just beginning."

I can't take it anymore, so much pretense and fear, said Agustín later on. I've completely lost myself. Reached the point of not knowing where life begins and theater ends, or even worse, where theater begins and life ends, where life begins to end with all this theater. The only thing left for me to do is go back to writing, the only reality that seriously belongs to me.

He would have to go to his apartment and face the situation, retrieve his clothes, his documents, and particularly his manuscripts. Above all retrieve that attempt at a novel he'd been debating with himself so long ago.

Long before the scene of the shot, which he no longer cared to dwell on. Forget it, lock it up for good. Grant it no more space in memory. Make it disappear. Nothing has happened here. Me, Argentine. Resorting to the usual remarks, catchwords of denial. How well he knew them. That was something else he didn't care to think about. *Basta.* Me, Argentine. No going back, no remembering or inquiring. New state and new story. As if the shot had been fired by another person, as if someone very Borgesian had been writing him.

"I want to pick up the pen again," he told Roberta, as if to say get a handle again on his life, if humanly possible.

"Good," Roberta answered. "Look, everything is put away at your place, except your manuscripts. I thought they might have some compromising stuff, you know? So I put them in a safe place."

"I need them now. Tell me where they are and I'll get them."

"Okay. They're where they belong. At the border. Between everyday life and that other life."

And without further explanation she gave him the coordinates for getting to You Know Where.

Then she left to find Bill.

You look like another person, said Bill when he saw her come in. And to cap it off he began treating her as if she were another person. Someone less close. What can I do for you? that non-committal sales pitch. Cut it out, Roberta complained soon enough. I haven't changed any more than your shop, look how orderly you've made it, where are the piles of clothes to roll around in? I wonder. Where did you put the mannequins disguised as old-fashioned ladies of distant galaxies? Besides, you've already seen me with short, dyed hair and in fact, if I'm not mistaken, participated in the cut. Yes, but now it's half grown-out, two-toned, you know? Don't do that to me, put on this wig, come back. Where? Anywhere, over here, next to me. No one ever comes back, you know, no one ever comes back to, more likely comes back from, like me, I'm coming back from. Nothing's changed in the shop, just got rid of excess stuff, the piles of clothes, since you weren't coming, they were useless, we're flourishing, more customers all the time, business on the upswing, I've had it, everyone buys their clothes here now, and now you come back from in over under above; I've had it. You don't want to see me, but you know I'm not coming back to and certainly not going back, never never back—I'm leaving. Don't provoke me, and listen—few things are more back than going away, it's the farthest back thing of all, going away, you turn around and bang, you show me your ass and I don't even feel like taking it, or even reaching out and touching it, no thanks—don't go, stay and tell me why you came if in fact you came for something. I wish I knew. You were gone too long. You're right, I look awful with my hair like this. Lend me the wig. Lend me that sweatshirt, it looks like mine. It doesn't look like it, it is it. What, the hair? Naturally, you look better now.

Better isn't the right word. No. Don't attack me, I came to play. You see, you see? one doesn't come to play, one just plays, something very different. I was very sick. I thought that something was going to grow between us, don't know why I never told you. Because you knew it was impossible. Is that why I didn't tell you? No, Bill, that's why you thought it.

While Roberta is entangled with Bill in a labored dialogue pursuing who knows what, Agustín is slowly making his way toward Ava Taurel's workplace to get his manuscripts. A novel he's afraid he won't be able to resume, marks of times gone by, virtually wiped out now by a shot he no longer wants to remember. Or wiped out by the desperate erasure of impotence, literary of course. Once more he is pursuing the quest for an ending that fails to appear, that gets transformed. But it's like circulating in a Calvino novel, with death the only ending. Okay. On with it. Ring the bell, speak to the fat, fat young woman with a talcum-powdered baby face who is sitting behind her fat receptionist desk and refuses to let him in without an appointment. But I'm not a client, I just came to get something that belongs to me. We don't call them clients, and everyone comes here to get something that belongs to them, something they've lost, their private ghosts—they come looking for what's missing, what they dream about and cry for.

The fat woman says none of this. Fatty simply smiles beatifically, a smile extending over that taut, ever so smooth, slightly transparent skin. Fatty knows that everyone is turned on in the end and surrenders despite initial scruples. No one rings that bell otherwise. Agustín persists. Call Ava Taurel, he says. Ava's with a slave, giving him his due, the receptionist answers in the sweetest of voices. But Ava has my manuscripts, she knows about this, I was told I could come for them. The gentleman is a writer, how lovely, you'll get lots of ideas here, ideas sometimes need a good thrashing, ideas sometimes blossom with the whip or even better with the willow rod, Ava will gladly loosen up your ideas, with blood as well, if you want, the receptionist persists without losing her aura. She's a blues singer, Ava will later say, a real angel. Truly, an angel who keeps extolling the benefits of the treatment.

Give in to your fantasies, man, act them out, then the fantasies will be grateful and come visiting you when you need them. No more blank pages, sprinkle them with your own blood. Or maybe you prefer an enema? Ava's an excellent nurse. She'll put on her uniform, inspect your ears, mouth, eyes, every orifice, she'll give you your enema with supreme imagination and meticulousness. I don't want an enema, I want my manuscripts, you may think they're one and the same thing, but. I don't think anything, you're the one who has to do the thinking here: do you like women's underwear? or maybe you prefer being enclosed in a cage for wild beasts and left there, suspended in midair, swaying till you can't stand it anymore and the dominatrices come and break you.

Agustín shuddered at the word *cage*. The fat woman, noting how he bristled from head to foot, stuck out the tip of her very pink tongue and passed it over her lips. Then with the tip of her tongue she displayed her tiny, sharp, perfect teeth. Come, she said finally, I'll give you a guided tour of the place, and before you know it you'll find something to your taste. Before you know it you'll even find your papers, but you yourself have to look for them. I'll show you the stocks where we suspend the men, the torture wheel, Ava's cubicle, everything.

And she led him down a long corridor lined with numerous closed doors.

"Keep your eyes open—we may find one of the dominatrices at work, something quite enlightening to see."

Agustín felt himself drawn along. As the fat woman opened the first door, she casually remarked, My name is Janet but they call me Baby Jane. And she let him enter first. Actually she pushed him into what looked like a simple little dressing room, somewhat turn-of-the-century and nostalgic in tone.

"This is the boudoir." (Evidently, Agustín said to himself.) "The drawers are filled with women's underwear, panties, bras, slips, garter belts, corsets, old-fashioned whalebone corsets. You see, many men enjoy wearing them. Sometimes I have to come and lace them up real tight. Tighter they ask, until they don't even have the breath to keep asking."

Agustín realized that he couldn't keep going. With one stroke he swept aside some fox skins, collapsed on the sofa, and said to the fat woman, now Baby Jane: "I've had it."

"Don't say that, sweetheart, we've just begun. You must have seen plenty of worse things."

"Exactly."

"Well, we can stay here until the bell rings. No one comes to this house by surprise."

"Not even the police?"

"The police least of all, they respect us." (Colleagues, thought Agustín.) "Listen, one time a complaint was lodged, a claim that men were being strangled here. But come, move a little closer. That's it. They claimed that we were strangling men, and the police descended and we had to give them permission to search the cubicles. They opened every door and asked the men who were being tended to, Are you okay? Yes, said the men as best they could, and then the police apologized and shut the door again. This is a free country, we serve only consenting adults, no one can object to that, we don't force anyone here to do anything they don't want to. So the police had to shut up and leave."

"They didn't ask for your papers?"

"No, what do you think? We're free citizens, we know our rights. They can't just kick us around. But they annoyed us plenty, showed up several days in a row, the girls lose their concentration and you can't work that way. It's a profession that demands the utmost attention. Finally the cops were convinced: no one was going to die here, and the boys in nooses were in sheer bliss."

"So the complaint was true?"

"What do you want me to say? Lots of men like that, and the dominatrices know just how far to squeeze."

"Just as the others do."

"What others, darling?"

"Doesn't matter."

"You seem very tense. Put on this corset. Put on these panties."

"You're crazy, Baby Jane."

"You'll relax, you'll see. Give in, let yourself go, surrender, and your worries will vanish. Many VIPs come here, business-men, they say they're fed up with responsibilities, with having to give orders all the time. Here we relieve them, here we give them the opportunity to let down their guard. They become children, invalids, women, dogs, whatever they want. The girls punish them for bad behavior, reward them when they're obe-dient. Put on one of these cute things. Ava is busy but I'll call the Puerto Rican girl—she has imagination and the longest nip-ples you've ever seen."

"And you?"

"I'm just the receptionist. Sometimes I give advice. Sometimes I have to console them when they're leaving. They like that, consolation. Me too; that's why I sing blues, songs that caress and hurt at the same time; not from pain, from sadness. Sad guys like you, I like those a lot. If you want, I'll put on a corset, as best I can, and you can hit me though I'd prefer not. I like gentle life, soft hands, velvets, cuddly things, affection."

"Like you."

"Or like your sweater. Let me touch it, it's so soft, so warm. You must be soft and warm too if you pull in your quills. One has to make love with you like porcupines do: with great care. You're full of bristles that I'll have to pull out one by one, you've even got a beard started; don't rub against my cheek or you'll irritate it, but you can rub against other parts if you want."

Agustín sank into the folds of Baby Jane's flesh, and as he explored and kissed her and tried to disappear in her, between those huge tits, those silky thighs, he was thinking of how to put it in more inspired words, something fleshier, warmed by the sun, sensual words that became banal as voluptuous pleasure entered another phase, warm and oozing, a custard of the soul, those corny tastes of the past, forgotten tastes resurfacing from the depths of yearning. Textures and scents of childhood without any demands.

How much do I owe you, he asked the fat woman, and the fat woman said to him, You're crazy, this isn't a whorehouse, what do you think, and he was stunned, not knowing what to do with his hands, his entire body gone limp. Let's go now, you have to find your manuscript, she told him. I don't want my manuscripts anymore, he answered. Some other day, she said then. Some other day, he repeated with considerable anticipation in his voice.

It was too late for him to return to his old apartment and reclaim some of his belongings from the person subletting it. Too late in the night and also in the general time of life. Going back for what? When going back would truly mean returning to Buenos Aires, to his childhood, to all of that. He went into a drugstore, bought a notebook and a ballpoint pen, and headed toward the Village looking for a café where he could sit and write. It was snowing very gently and not too cold a night. He was grateful for having had the strength that afternoon to buy some rubber boots, woolen socks, grateful for Roberta's fleece-lined raincoat, which was rather tight on him, grateful for other things without specifying them. So few cars, such silence. A dense, oatmeal silence, a calmness Agustín couldn't have imagined in New York before living there. A city calm and friendly as well, with crisscrossing currents of unrestrained fantasy and beauty. The snow reduced the contrasts, the snow powdered everything with an iridescence under which even the garbage bags disappeared, and they were huge black plastic bags, like those used to carry soldiers' bodies after the war. Agustín was a soldier after the war, a soldier's corpse in a huge plastic bag, white in this case.

Only the mad and the desperate wander around the streets on a night like this, he said to himself. He was approaching the Village, would soon be getting lost in the winding tree-lined streets of sedate homes, where people would be walking their dogs and frisking in the snow. But he was still a few blocks away, and one among the desperate many approached him for a coin. He didn't have one, thought the guy was going to knife him and almost hoped that he would: an easy out, the simplest way of ending it all, including the cowardliness of being unable to do so with his own hand.

The man didn't even pause to insult him but went on his way, slipping and staggering in the snow. Agustín laughed at his own apprehensions, recalled Baby Jane, the ridiculous garter belt with lace trim that had tagged the romance, laughed a bit harder, and entered the first café he found. He wanted to sit down and write before his laughter ran out. Before he began brooding again.

Inside a story from childhood is another story without an ending, of a woman walking on the top floor with all her encephalic matter exposed. She has an ax in her hand and is looking for revenge. Don't go near that woman, don't go into abandoned houses in the woods. He remembered the house offered him in the Adirondacks, surrounded by woods, where the woman with the encephalic matter might be waiting for him, against whom no weapon at all could defend him. He'd bought a revolver and had defended himself against another woman who had no intention at all of assault but maybe just wanted to hit on him. What a bleak story, what a shitty fate. Between Baby Jane's breasts, nestled beneath her armpits, buried in her adiposities and folds and moist areas, he had felt protected. There the lurking dangers were make-believe: whips and cages and willow rods and needles and nipple clips and loops for squeezing the testicles, but that's as far as it went.

How can you expect me to enjoy voluntary sexual torture when I come from a country where people were tortured for alleged political reasons, for the sheer horror of it, with desperate, not at all compliant victims? How do you expect me to enjoy it or even be interested in it? What I need is to know why someone becomes a torturer, a murderer, to know why an upright citizen can one day unawares be transformed into a monster.

Sentences barely intuited, maybe heard from somebody else,

questions impossible to frame aloud, much less to Baby Jane with her air of innocence.

He opened the notebook with the idea of jotting down something on innocence. Innocence to be found in the sewers of the world. But he wrote none of that, giving way instead to ruminations on the inner life, with garbled confessions and vague associations—aware as he wrote of not having to decipher them until much later on.

To write about the immediate, almost an impossible task. One's arm must extend way beyond its reach in order to touch what is virtually clinging to one's body. What long-distance arm did he need just to reach Roberta, to brush her cheek? Roberta, so very, very close to him, virtually him.

The writing that cannot be written, the embrace that is not given, the kiss one is ever fleeing without realizing it.

He recalled a story of Roberta's, a true story. She'd never managed to write it, like many others, capsules of life that she stored and sometimes repeated aloud, unable to find the necessary distance to transfer them to paper.

He would write Roberta's story for her, at least this minimal story that didn't involve him—Roberta and the beggar as she had told it to him—practically hearing Roberta's voice, whereupon it would no longer be something written, unraveled; it would continue being that magma of literalness, that which does not yet yield to the noble status of metaphor. The beggar had approached Roberta on a corner, when she was chatting with a certain friend she'd just run into. The beggar, covered with rags and reeking of cheap booze, asked for some money to keep on drinking. Roberta, who appreciated his honesty but also wanted to get rid of him, gave him a crisp dollar bill. The beggar, overcome by emotion and wanting to reciprocate such generosity, held out a crushed, frayed cigarette. Roberta said, No thanks, I don't smoke, whereupon the beggar, enveloped in the stench of alcohol, persisted in attempting to thrust the cigarette in her hand. Roberta, thinking that the cigarette was potentially useful to him, while for her it was a mere smidgen of tobacco on its way to the garbage can, repeated, Thanks, I don't smoke. The beggar's eyes filled with tears, his face screwed up like a baby's, and Roberta, deeply moved, put her hand on his shoulder and told him, Honestly, I don't smoke. The grimy creature, with that noble human face, broke into tears and tried to fling himself into Roberta's arms. She fled in panic, but to this day could never, ever forgive herself for that rejection.

Sitting over his notebook at the café table, Agustín likewise found the story painful, at a juncture when he himself had not been rejected but despite everything accepted. Imagine, being welcomed by Baby Jane. Better not to think of that incident. That place where all sorts of weapons were within reach, and he had not wanted to use any of them. Or had not been able to. Not even the one that that Mother-bitch Nature had provided him with—not a weapon, quite the opposite, but still. Like the ax of the executioner? He left the money for his coffee on the table and stood up without looking at the waitress. A skinny girl. So many skinny females walking around when there are those cushiony ones beckoning.

At least at Roberta's there's a down comforter. And good heat and a bed. Especially a bed.

"What did Ava say to you? Did you get your manuscripts?"

"I didn't see her and didn't get them and would rather not think about what brings you to places like that."

"True. Why go looking for literature in the most sordid places when literature comes to you right at home, all by yourself?"

"Quit your—"Agustín started to complain, but wound up falling asleep on the unmade bed wearing his rubber boots and huddled up on the quilt.

Roberta pulled off his boots, secretly hoping to wake him, but he simply clutched the tangled sheets and moved away from her.

Where is love in all of this? Roberta asked herself again, like an echo.

And she settled down in front of the television to watch a movie. And another, and if necessary possibly a third.

When the bell started ringing, she paid no attention, thinking it part of the film. But the ring became more persistent. Who is it? she asked, frightened, approaching the door. A familiar voice said, I hear the TV, you're not asleep, open up. And Roberta opened the door to find Bill standing practically on top of her, with his huge smile, all dark and wonderful, exactly as his mother had brought him into the world but considerably more developed. You're naked, exclaimed Roberta.

"That I am. I've got nothing to put on. I'm looking for a stack of clothes, piles of them. Times have changed, you know, but I miss the past."

"I'm not alone."

"I don't care."

"Where are your clothes?"

"In the incinerator. I burned my bridges."

"You're nuts. Now what?"

She let him in for the time being. Agustín was sound asleep and unaware of all the activity. They raised the volume on the TV, turned off the only light, and began embracing on the couch until Roberta said, Hey, I have a stack of clothes, come on.

And she led him into the walk-in closet she knew intimately. There they remained the rest of the night.

Roberta emerged from the closet when Agustín was already awake. We have visitors, she said.

The two men sized each other up from afar, like two boxers, like two fighting cocks. Then they sat down at the table and together had the breakfast Roberta had prepared.

"You're one of Roberta's characters, come out of the closet of her mind?"

"Definitely not. Nor am I one of *your* characters. I'm simply the spy who came out of the cold, if you like."

Surprisingly Agustín felt not threatened but relieved. At least he was being recognized as a writer, that was something. They went on talking about other subjects, as if Roberta and Bill hadn't spent half the night in the closet, as if Bill weren't wearing a pair of Roberta's jeans that were ridiculously short on him.

Anyone care for another cracker, a bit of marmalade? Roberta kept asking, like the consummate housekeeper she was far from being, and the two men accepted, ate with considerable appetite considering the circumstances, with Roberta pressing solicitously, I'll make more coffee, maybe you'd like some orange juice.

Bill told them how he was taking total charge of the boutique, transforming it into an antiques shop: Well, you know, old but beautiful things. Maybe Roberta and Agustín had something they wanted to sell, they could leave it on consignment.

"We're not from here," said Roberta. "What do you expect us to have? One of the dramas of exile, or at least of the wandering life, is that it hinders accumulation. There are so many things I'd like to have, but then I ask myself what to do with them at the next move. You never know where you're going to wind up. That's why I can only allow myself a tapestry, a work of art you can roll up and put under your arm. The rest has to be disposable. A disposable life, it's not funny."

Bill asked, "What is exile?"

"Exile is knowing that you'll never again return to the place you belong."

"But both of you can return to your country. There are no more problems, that I know of. They have democracy now."

"Yes, of course, that we can, but I don't know if return is possible. Things change. Not all roads can be retraced."

"Besides, there's an exile from oneself, more inevitable than appears at a glance."

"Which reminds me," said Bill, leaping to his feet; he rushed to the front door, opened it, and vanished.

Agustín looked at Roberta questioningly. What does all this mean? said his raised eyebrows. Roberta puffed out her cheeks. The air escaped noisily through her pursed lips. Involuntarily. Sorry, she said, for the noise but perhaps for the other thing. I think that I'm, she babbled, but couldn't go on. I think that I'm very desperate, was the remark, and she couldn't finish it because at that very moment Bill entered with a bundle of clothes under his arm and, inside the bundle, shoes. He sat down on the bed to put on his socks and then the shoes. I won't tie the laces, I'm going to the bathroom to change. Sorry, he said.

Agustín ignored him. I have no rights over you, I've screwed up your life enough, he said to Roberta as though Bill didn't exist.

He didn't say, I'm going, you're free. He didn't say it, but he moved into action, quickly so as not to have second thoughts, throwing on the rest of his clothes.

From the doorway, he quoted a well known tango: "It's my turn today to beat a retreat."

Roberta did nothing to stop him.

9

Roberta and Bill were alone in her house for the first time. He began nosing around in every corner. Spare but attractive, he said. Neat, he added, implying something else in view of the prevailing disorder. I like it, I like you; you've got all sorts of secrets, yet I feel very close to you.

That's it, replied Roberta, for that's how it was with Bill, everything tipped either to the other side or this one, the side she was currently inhabiting.

Whistling softly, Bill wandered about with his typical ease, like someone who'd spent his entire life there. He picked up the books left on the table and set them on the bookshelves, retrieved garments from the floor and began folding them to put on a chair, carried the breakfast dishes into the kitchen, scooped up the crumbs from the table, began arranging papers.

"Don't touch my papers!" Roberta shouted. He looked at her. She backed off.

"Sorry," she said. "I'm on edge. I don't know. I just don't know. I'd like to escape from all this. If I go away, do I take the papers? Do you think I'll ever write again? I was supposed to be a writer once, did you know? But I haven't written for so long."

"Don't leave. No one, in fact, ever leaves for good. Remember, you yourself told me that. I don't want you to go away, I want to know you better. Tell me about yourself."

"When I was little, I had a very proper family and an aunt who was sort of crazy. Sort of crazy and sort of an aunt, you could say. She was my mother's cousin, very young, and was always hanging around the house. I think she was sort of in love with my father, that man with the pipe. Solemn fellow. Everything was sort of, you see. But in revenge, I'd say, my sort-of aunt, who never did things halfway, read me the scariest stories she could find. So that I would eat, she said. I disliked my aunt's stories or liked them too much and that's why I began writing, I think, to invent my own stories. Which I sort of like. Which also scare me. Where I wonder does tenderness come into all this?"

"Here," said Bill, grasping her hand and putting it on an interesting section of anatomy. His.

Roberta went for it. For a long while her pores, all of her lips, her innermost recesses, her soul, oozed with tenderness, she remembered the soul, that quivering presence without a presence, she felt warm surges of tenderness transformed into a sweet little creature coursing through her veins, she allowed herself to be flooded by tenderness until she could no longer endure those forgotten sensations and pushed Bill slightly away, slipping out slightly more from underneath him.

"Let me breathe," she implored.

Then she realized that she wasn't imploring him but rather circumstances, and she burst into tears. Bill said nothing, took her in his arms, held her against his chest, and began caressing her, until she said, Let me go, he'll be coming back, and he asked her, Are you afraid? and she realized that she was, panic-stricken, not of Agustín but of her own absence of feeling, at not having been afraid of him during that entire period, at having allowed herself to be swept along by someone else's desperation.

She tried to tell Bill something that wasn't a lie but an explanation.

"Agustín and I embarked on a rough adventure, a probing investigation, stirring up lots of shit, exposing all the ghosts that we could, entering forbidden areas, searching for the unnamable. I believe we needed an answer and there are no answers, questions always lead to other questions—I don't know, I feel terribly wounded, remote from everything, removed."

"You two were writing a play."

"Yes. No. On and off, afterward I don't know."

"Tell me about it, if you can."

"There's a murder, I believe. Of a woman. At first I thought the victim was a man, but it turned out to be a woman and then I no longer understood anything. Why she had to be killed, nothing. But he insisted. I still don't understand. She was young and pretty, terrific."

"Like you."

Roberta looked at him fixedly. For a long while. His eyes were almost green, with bright flecks, unusual in such a dark-skinned face. She kept looking at him as if wanting to plunge into those eyes and forget the rest.

"Yes, like me," she agreed finally in a very low voice. And added, "Killing isn't so hard after all, is it?"

10

Agustín is standing on a short line at the money machine, completely caught up in apprehension again, confused, unable to recall the number that would open doors to the treasure hunt.

The code? Deposited in Roberta's hands and forgotten. Roberta the fairy godmother. Damn it. She'd been taking care of these chores lately, paying bills, organizing his life by mail. Enough of that. The coffers might very well be empty, with him standing there like an idiot letting a woman—that woman—handle accounts as if his accounts were, God knows what. Little genie, little genie, one, two, tric, trac, give me the number, don't let it slip my mind, little genie, the open sesame of Ali Baba's cave, hah, tell it to me, one two three four that wasn't it—what could they be, little genie? My turn's coming and I can't remember, I only remember—

His turn has now come but he steps aside and stands there, at one side, to regain his memory. And that swine, memory, plays dirty tricks on him. Not a single number, the combination. Not a number in his memory—London Bridge is falling down, falling down, can I get through? You'll get through, you will, but the last one won't. Detained. De-tained. No. Please. Make a getaway, escape. By your wits. Remember the days when you first arrived, when every act seemed liberating and a ball. A ball. Like those places you dance in until you collapse, but he didn't dance. No. Roberta had taken him to those places. Danger without danger. Other women had taken him too. Had to drag him, practically; he didn't dance but the dance floor did, it kept getting larger, the walls opening up, the walls dancing, and sometimes there were rhythmical curtains or sliding panels merging with the dance of the others, not his because he didn't dance, just looked on as the lights transformed the others into one vast multiple being. He with no urge to shake himself much, just wanting, trying, hoping to belong, and at times it was under a starry, translucent dome, with dancing planetary projections and stars flecking the floor and the walls, a universe madly twirling making him whirl, he without any desire to move, not feeling his feet on the floor now or on the dome or walls, whirling to the rhythm of galloping projected stars. Or it would happen in tunnels. Deep, unfathomable abandoned subway tunnels, pierced by other tunnels of light, lasers tracing their nonexistent geometry of colors, their holographic reality.

(Later, memory would transform Agustín into a hologram of an unconscious repeated motion, a motion he doesn't recall having made, yet he is imprinted by it and knows it was made: his right hand slipping into a pocket, taking out a revolver, and raising it to a temple. His right hand drawing a revolver toward a temple. Hand, revolver, temple. The motion has been completed though he sometimes divides it in fragments. He knows that in each portion of memory, in each minimal molecule, that complete motion exists with all its complete consequences. An inexplicable movement that was initiated perhaps in the distant days of his childhood and culminated on that fateful day, if it has indeed culminated.)

In the bank, only recollections of the dance. But he does not dance. He stands gravely to one side as the party proceeds, right there, by the cash machines, because some mad or perhaps inspired friend of Roberta's—or possibly some other woman from an unspecified time—had dreamed up the idea of celebrating his birthday in this very forbidden yet accessible place. A magnetic card was all you needed, so they all entered the bank with bottles of champagne and cans of beer and ghetto blasters and even a cake with candles. At eleven P.M., to avoid running into too many customers, they celebrated a birthday and waited for the strike of midnight, expecting to be kicked out at any moment. An act mildly subversive, with the banks's TV surveillance cameras aimed at them. Nobody came around, and what a surprise security would have next day when they checked the tapes, but undoubtedly no one ever looked at them if the alarm didn't go off.

New York was the most wonderful city in the world when he first arrived. Someone once asked him: Where would you have chosen to live in the time of the Roman Empire, when it was in full decadence, at its greatest decline? In Rome, naturally, he'd replied, as if to say New York at the end of the twentieth century, crumbling and celebrating at the same time. A time to be alive, a perpetual rebuilding of the world. And now—

A hand touched his shoulder and Agustín felt it through Roberta's absurd fleece-lined raincoat. A gentle hand.

"Don't you feel well? Can I help you, get you a glass of water?"

Barely turning his head, Agustín saw an open, pale face—diaphanous, he said to himself, the word is diaphanous—haloed with frothy woolen scarves woven in pastel colors. In one of those leaps of memory, those flashes of escaping the moment he'd been having lately, he thought this figure might well be the positive, the white, utterly feminine version of the bum trying to be his own feminine version, that summer in Washington Square, enveloped in a long dress of variegated squares knitted by himself, dancing to whatever rhythm someone was playing at that moment. She—the woman at the bank—was very calm, very sweet, insisting, Do you need anything? Shall I give you a hand? Shall I? Do you need? Agustín was about to say yes when the signs popped into his head: DO NOT LEND YOUR CARD TO ANYONE FOR ANY REASON. DO NOT ALLOW ANOTHER PERSON TO INSERT YOUR CARD IN THE SLOT FOR YOU. DO NOT LET ANYONE KNOW YOUR CODE NUMBER. Tell not, lend not, explain not, request not, allow not, tell not. He least of anyone.

"Nothing, thanks. I had a dizzy spell. I don't need anything, thank you. I'm okay."

Actually he needed everything and it showed in his face. She, with her opaline-blue eyes, the diaphanousness of her golden braids twirled around like earmuffs, would not be rebuffed. "Look, you aren't well. Let's have a coffee right across the street—your sugar level must be very low."

Her presence seemed to calm Agustín's anxiety. He made a vague gesture of moving toward the machines; she stayed at a discreet distance and he, facing the screen, finally hit on the right colored numbers and got the bills. Green.

They went to the café to celebrate. She seemed surprised when he, terrified, turned down the invitation to go upstairs to her place, just above the café, a step away.

Two floors up, the climb won't kill you. No, no, quite the contrary, he answered incongruously while sipping an ultra-Cuban *café con leche* and gathering his wits.

Divested of scarves and coat, she revealed a long, luminous neck, and with long, slender hands began unfurling a *sfogliatella* as she described the seductions of her home to Agustín.

"You must come and meet Rosie, my tame rat. She's a beauty. I rescued her from the lab; they were going to vivisect her and she looked so sweet. She has a little pink snout and is big now, bigger than the rats that run by you in the park. I feed her well, her coat is shiny, I don't give her junk food and french fries and leftovers like the other rats eat. Rosie is vegetarian. What do you do in real life?"

"I'm a writer," Agustín confessed in spite of himself, choking a bit on his croissant. "Omnivorous," he added.

"I work for the Museum of Natural History. I wanted to do taxidermy but after a while didn't like it, very dirty work. Now I make small animals for them. You should see, they turn out to look so natural. Come to the house, I'll show you my cockroaches, the nest of mice peeking out under my bed. They're beauties."

"You too. You're a beauty, I mean. But don't ask me up. No, I can't, it's not a good idea, I shouldn't, no."

He picked up the check to pay on the way out and left without saying goodbye.

He had to learn again to manage on his own in the city. In the world. No one could help him, not Baby Jane so sweet in the midst of all that shit, or this sweet girl offering him a hand, or even Roberta, who when it came to giving a hand went overboard, elbow-deep. Worse, up to her neck. And now she was withdrawing. Withdrawing her body, a body that stood for writing and everything that really counts. He'd go to her house and thank her and tell her that her sacrifice was no longer needed, that from now on he'd take care of himself and he was sorry for the trouble he'd caused her but could they please remain friends because he had no friends here.

He entered with his key and found Roberta and Bill in bed side by side, modestly covered up, sheets drawn up to their noses, two pairs of rather cheery eyes peering out.

"Excuse me, I didn't mean to disturb you."

"Come right in. Make yourself at home."

He accepted the invitation, ignored the irony in Roberta's voice—perhaps the irony wasn't even there—threw himself down on the couch and began removing his boots, but then checked himself. I just dropped by for a minute, and have to leave right away. I needed a bit of friendly warmth, he said.

And Bill, so utterly at ease in his own skin, guiltless, unrepentant, decided to step into the picture and offer his help. Not out of concern but to be of indirect help to Roberta.

"If there's anything I can do?"

"If anything has to be done, I have to do it myself, thanks. And I say thanks in all sincerity, not as a rejection. Thanks."

"Okay."

Roberta involuntarily shifted the roles.

"Turn around, Agustín, I'm getting out of bed. I'll fix Bloody Marys. I think we can all use one."

(Later she'd remark to Bill: Poor Gus, I dislodged him from

my bed with one stroke of the pen, just when he was becoming a little more human. And Bill pointed out the obvious, that a little more human isn't altogether human, and that if she had dislodged him so easily, it meant he'd already been dislodged.)

They had their drinks in silence. Then Roberta told Agustín, Go ahead and do what you have to, but come by for me tonight, Lara's having a party and you're expected.

Over Roberta's shoulder Agustín could see Bill making the bed, very self-possessed. Maybe that's why he said, Yes, I'll come by for you at around seven; let's go to Lara's. You and me.

Lay off, Agustín, I'm fed up with you—this she doesn't say. She simply tells him, *Basta*. Not intending to say even that, not another word, case closed.

To avoid having to answer to his laments, Roberta wanted to make going to Lara's together seem quite casual.

I don't drag you anywhere, you go because you want to, because you're invited—she doesn't say this either, refusing to get more involved in his intrigues. And thinking also: Enough of letting myself get entrapped. No more playing his mother, screw him, kick him in the ass, son of a bitch, shake him off on the way to Lara's as they're crossing the winding streets of Tribeca.

Watch it—she doesn't say—don't get knocked over by cars heading for the tunnel. Sometimes I think I ought to leave Manhattan, get away from the island. And she later says, unable to hold it back: You know, you two are not at all interchangeable, and I'm not bringing you along just because my blackie, as you call him, can't go. I'm not bringing you or dragging you, we just happen to be going to the same party, if you recall. I don't need anyone to escort me anywhere, she forgets to add, for she had forgotten it, too, her non-neediness having been lodged over many long months in the the need of the other.

After reaching the entrance to Lara's building, and being let in by someone who led them to a huge freight elevator, Roberta begins to feel herself recovering, not like someone recuperating from a long, obscure illness but rather, retrieving a long-lost object.

And she tells Agustín, Let's pretend we're writing with the body again, let's put it into words, how about it?

We're in a black cage going up a black tunnel and are birds impaled against the walls.

it's a roofless, chain-drawn cage

some stranger operates the chains, pulling and pulling on the chains, in a tremendous effort to hoist us up

we're going up the shaft of a vertical mine, never to find the lode, there is no such lode in which case no mine

there is no lode. Let's never use the word again. Nor the word 'mine'. Remember that, The Mine Shaft. They had to shut it down because it was atrociously unsanitary. The chains. Those who were going to have themselves punished and beaten with chains

chained for life. If we begin to censor words, I'm the one who would have to say no, and I can't

okay. Let's keep going. Now the lever will be pressed by this ascending Charon who hasn't said boo and God knows what language he speaks, and the door will open onto the treasure grove.

Heavy, massive metal doors, the only access to the other territory, Lara's loft.

Fairyland, they might have exclaimed in unison when they stepped out of the black freight elevator were it not for their lingering respect for language, their attempt at least to avoid purple prose. Fairyland, they might have exclaimed and, unsettling, too, which was much easier to say. For unsettling it was— that flickering of an inverted sky, composed of candles, little ones and big ones, votive candles and candles for candelabra, some with colored drippings, the residue of other eons in Lara's boundless space.

"You didn't pay the electricity bill again."

"Roberta, the great disappeared."

(No, not that word, please, even in English.)

Overlapping voices: Roberta's sounding ironic, Lara's dominating, and Agustín's pleas barely audible, and hardly relevant since he alluded to other circumstances in another land.

Lara was presiding in the kitchen over a steaming, glittering caldron. Adding aromatic herbs and talking incessantly as she stirred. Uttering not incantations but invitations: Help yourself to some vodka, we're going Russian today—there's beef Stroganoff or something resembling it, I hope. Hey, Roberta, you missed the poetry, this is indirect, magical lighting. Oh yes, they want to evict me, but this time they haven't cut off the electricity, as if I cared. They want to evict all of us in the building, which is getting lovelier day by day, you'll see. Pass the wine please, not for me but for the stew. Oh yeah, I've changed the decor completely, you'll see for yourselves. I have a winter garden now, everyone's out there."

"Everyone?" Agustín whispered in terror. "Must be a battalion from the size of the pot."

"A man who mumbles. Watch out for that type."

"Watch out for the pol—"

"Yes, yes," interrupted the ever ready scout dormant in Roberta. "Yes, Magoo says we must watch out for pollution, politicians, pollinators, poltergeists."

"No danger of that. The house is well protected. Thanks to Glenn. Guardian of the spirit, they call him. Glenn is in the winter garden. You'll see, I installed it after finding some divine little antique wicker chairs in the street. I find everything in the street—what gifts the city has bestowed on me! Roberta, tell that guy to stop muttering, and to keep his eyes open. Soon he'll be writing about everything he finds here. My decor, as you know, is constantly transformed in the course of time and of my wanderings. This new sculpted piece, for example: I found one of those old-fashioned toilet tanks, remember? from the days pull chains were used, a marvel, and I attached a Brazilian *figa* amulet to it as a Brazilian pull, a penis to entice certain young fellows who frequent this retreat. Don't you love the chorus girl legs of those cardboard dolls peeping out of the tank? I found them, too, in a pile of trash one night when we were doing the rounds with Jack—poor Jack, he brought me luck, he used to find all sorts of treasures in urban garbage, he found everything, everything; a bit too much, let me tell you, he found garbage-pile people as well, to use and to abuse. In the end, he died, true to his spirit, as they say, though it may be such a new spirit that no one has yet figured out how to harness it. Jack was determined to save himself, but no one escapes. Jack knew how to find things but he ran into the other thing. Retrovirus, they call it, just ask Hector Bravo. One night Jack and I found at a corner what looked like a pile of rags, but they were treasures. Velvets that I used to make a canopy for the bed. I'll show it to you some other time. We can't go into my bedroom today because the papers are all in the order they fell. Glenn says that you must respect the order—"

"I have to leave."

"—in which papers fall. Hey, don't run away. As a writer you must know about that. The order of written papers is the order of the world. I'm writing a novel myself. Dictated to me by voices, I'm a channel, it's unbelievable. Glenn taught me to pay attention to my voices."

"I believe I heard. Mention of him, of Glenn, I mean."

"Sure, he's very famous—You'll meet him, Bobbie, he was Madonna's psychic."

"Maradona, the soccer player?"

"Soccer is and will always be nonsense, I know."

"Madonna. Stop teasing. Glenn is an extraordinary man, the purest, I don't know what I'd do without him. He neutralizes the charge of all the objects I find on the street, he says they're very highly charged with bad vibes and that's why Jack died."

"From what you've said, it wasn't exactly the objects that were charged."

"There are no subjects anymore."

"You two are impossible. One can't tell you anything. You confuse everything. But you're not going to confuse me. I know where things stand, that's why I put those gargoyles that I rescued from a demolition over there, so that—"

Or rescued from a collapse, Agustín felt like adding but decided to keep silent, as was often the case. To keep silent so as to try to hear/to not hear those voices that almost never said the expected, and this time it was Lara's voice, running on and on, tracing the contours of her own terror of the vacuum

"—they would smile at me."

Every inch of the vast expanse of the loft—broken by the typical row of cast-iron columns—conveyed a setting both childlike and somewhat perverse, a magical circle of clowns and monsters in which little wooden horses and omnivorous beasts consorted in a transformist rite, in which a leopard's head with bloody jaws, for example, provided a cushion to rest one's own tame head.

Lara kept moving along verbally and physically through her world of reflections. The pot simmered away from afar, performing its task of slow-fire cookery.

And this figure is also one of Jack's sculptures, Lara explained. It's my guardian angel. It's an Oruro devil mask given me by a Bolivian who had to return to his country with much less luggage than he brought. And these carvings are from my Haitian friend, maybe we'll find him in back—I don't know if he came or not, some people feel so at home here they come without saying hello, settle in, do whatever they want, and my Haitian friend exchanged these carvings—fabulous, aren't they?—for seven saxophones that he used for who knows what and I can't even remember where I got them. But there were seven, seven saxophones, and I think the carvings are worth it.

Look.

No, that's nothing, don't distract him, I want to introduce you to Frieda. You'll say she's a puppet, but take a good look at her: Frieda's alive. I had her hanging over my bedroom dresser and she didn't let me sleep, she kept making me get out of bed to put necklaces and perfume on her, or to bundle her up when it was cold. She wouldn't even let me listen to my voices, it was crazy. Glenn suggested I burn her in a great auto-da-fé but I refused to do it. For once I didn't listen to Glenn and sometimes I think I made a mistake. Anyhow, Frieda isn't mine, she belongs to Ratcliff, a sensational guy, you'll meet him when we get to the back—come around this way. Rat has a house in the country filled with puppets. An abandoned house full of puppets, just imagine, exposed to the elements, where puppets coming from the heat of Sicily experience firsthand the Massachusetts climate. All the puppets you can imagine and not one like my Frieda. Frieda is complete, even has her own little cunt, just look. She's alive.

Whereupon Lara lifted Frieda's skirts. And burst out laughing, her delicate features contorting and her heavy mane of hair tossing in the candlelight.

Agustín pressed Roberta's hand. Who knows, she thought, this may be a little too heavy for him first time out. Or too rich.

Lara kept moving along with Frieda in her arms, all talked out by now. The silence made Agustín dizzy and he clung to Roberta's hand and followed her inside, submissively, along pathways of candles. Like in a spooky children's story, he told himself as they approached the so-called winter garden, bounded by the classic white picket fence.

Seated in a circle like the Lady of the Unicorn were the other guests. Those who had been mentioned and others: the one named Glenn, the one by the name of Ratcliff, someone called Abbie, and those who hadn't had the good fortune to be singled out by Lara. Just shadows, total unknowns.

Is this the movie I'm supposed to get back into? Agustín wondered when Roberta let go of his hand, nudging him through the open gate of the fence. Is this the scene I must become a part of in order to reestablish an order that can never be reestablished in me? Could this be order?

Glenn, from his white wicker chair, treasure of urban trash, turned his glance toward Agustín, hesitating at the entrance, and answered his unspoken questions with another question, in Hasidic manner: Why so many questions without answers? he said with a trace of a smile, allowing Agustín to advance a couple of steps and join the circle.

Over here. Glenn patted the artificial grass, inviting Agustín to be seated. Here, on the shaggy green carpet, as if it were the softest of lawns.

Roberta, her hand freed, sank into a folding chair under the nonshade of a dried-up palm tree. Outside, it had begun snowing; languorous flakes danced by the windows and silence seeped into the so-called winter garden, more wintry than ever.

Seated on the floor, Agustín pulled up his knees, encircled them with his arms, and rested his head in that nest as though he were crying. Roberta stroked his hair lightly, forgetting her sound resolutions.

The others found this contagious.

And in the midst of that noncrying, that insinuation or remembrance of tears, Glenn's voice began to rise, intoning something over his tureen-like Chinese singing bowls, over that soup of dense, nourishing sounds, at times murky and at times clear.

Only Roberta noted Agustín's shudder, and said to herself, It was that damned soup's fault, like someone misreciting a tango and compounding the mistake, for Agustín's associations had wandered off to much vaster regions, likewise murky and clear. His Río de la Plata, where the drowned sometimes floated to the surface. Why had Glenn's vaguely suggestive singing bowls evoked such memories of other times? Memories like corpses that are like memories, and someone had slit open their bellies so that they would sink, and someone had thrown them still alive perhaps from army helicopters, and one didn't want to, doesn't want to know about those memories. He had been there during that period, must have known about it before they were memories but reali—

Agustín Palant, a man's voice interrupted, bringing him back with both his first and second names to the here and now of Lara's house. Agustín Palant, repeated the voice, extending an inner consultation. Your name rings a bell. Are you by any chance the author of that truly memorable novel about the perfectible escape?

It's probable, Agustín would have replied had he retained a jot of his former humor. Or he might have answered, Indubitable, or something equally evasive in response to the man who was telling him how memorable his forgettable novel was.

Humorlessly, listlessly, he answered, Yes, the easiest reply in the world, and felt surprised, as if his answer had been another of the infinite yeses of falsehood.

The questioner heard none of his surprise and began talking nonstop, like the robot inhabitants of Lara's space. I'm a critic and an admirer of your work, I recall such and such passages—you are worthy of being ranked with so-and-so and such and such, great masters of Latin American literature, which along with eastern Europe literature, in my opinion, blah, blah, and I see your novel as kindred to the great, distinguished art of the modern novel—what a coincidence running into you here, but I always say that in Lara's mansion, and you know I say this with no sarcasm—sarcasm is not my nature, I want you to know—I always say that in this mansion of Lara's one encounters the most extraordinary subjects and objects. It is truly a castle of wonders, you know, nothing Kafkaesque about it, I don't speak in metaphors like you writers.

But the pot, at that moment, did. From the other end of the vast universe of the loft, its effluvia wafted an olfactory metaphor. I believe the hour for beef Stroganoff has struck, someone remarked, and the others began purring hungrily.

The critic, displaced as the center of attention, tried to enlist the complicity of the unknown woman who had arrived with Agustín Palant—his wife apparently, judging by the blank gaze his own pithy comments had elicited in her.

"You will note," he said in Roberta's ear, "that the mistress of the house is oblivious to her guests' hunger. She must be listening to her voices. The more drugs, the more voices. She says that they're dictating a novel to her and she is writing and writing. Glenn encourages her. That man's a menace, and not just for literature, for I had an opportunity to glance at Lara's manuscripts and they're mere doodlings. Graphically beautiful, I won't deny, but illegible, totally senseless doodlings."

And he added loudly, "Wake up, Lara, wake up. Stop listening to your voices, heed the growling of our empty stomachs."

Lara seemed to know him well, and simply said, Pragmatic starvelings, victuals will be at the disposal of your insatiable gullet shortly. And thereupon she strode regally toward the dark corner of the unending loft, behind the columns, to light the remaining candles. The table sprang into view, laid with a profusion of lace, adorned with gilt candelabra and pale, rather limp roses like flowers on a hat.

No way of escaping theater, thought Agustín three seconds before Roberta whispered to him, Chinese time boxes: we're smack in the middle of what looks like a replay of a sixties imitation of *fin de siècle* decadence.

Good food and wine performed their alchemical transmutation. Everyone except the Ratcliff person was speaking at once, until someone began speaking for him and told about his project of setting the Statue of Liberty afloat so that Bronx inhabitants might also enjoy it.

"No," Ratcliff was quick to correct. "I proposed mounting the statue on a raft, with a tug to tow it out to sea and take it as far out as necessary whenever its presence became disturbing. It was a good project but the city didn't approve it. I've lost interest in it. Now I want everything at a standstill, stagnant, dead."

"He requested a death certificate. It too was denied."

"Impossible in this country to have ideas."

"It's logical he would demand peace and quiet, with all those puppets."

"I took a few for myself, to rescue them, but Frieda was the only—"

"Anyway, what does he want with a death certificate? He's as good as dead already."

"They bug you for taxes, don't want you to die, so that you can pay."

Roberta poured herself another glass of wine.

"And you," Glenn suddenly asked her, "why that tiny speck of fear in the depths of your eyes? Or maybe it's modesty and not fear."

"I'd like to know that myself. You could be the one to tell

me, you seem to have a lot of the poet—I'm just a humble novelist."

"A novelist. How nice," the critic chimed in. "Structured people, novelists. May I ask the ultimate New York question: What are you working on now? Perhaps you'll be presenting us with a new novel soon?"

" 'Presenting' may not be the way to put it. What can I say? I'm afraid instead I'll be clobbering you with one. No. Let's say I'm working on a play. Let's say I'm an integral part of the work."

"Are you an actress as well?"

"Not at all. I just let myself live. In this city of sheer theater."

In this city of sheertheater. In this city of sheerthe— She let the phrase bounce around in her head, bang, bang, right and left, like the clapper of a bell—"sheertheater"—like the Chinese gongs, bang, and tried to keep it that way. She fled to the bathroom, just as Lara was proclaiming, "Theater, you said it, baby. It's time to move on. We must go upstairs to see the great Edouard. They're waiting for us."

Roberta shut the door, craving the privacy of the most private spot in any house. A refuge, almost a vice, for her lately.

A place to sit and think in streams, or force out ideas under pressure, for ideas can easily be flushed away afterward.

And to think that I used to love this city, she said to herself as she groped for the light switch. It was a live, protean city, and now I'm left with only its darkest side as sheerthe—ater, she added almost aloud, startled when the light went on.

Because this was Lara's bathroom, where introspection could run only along the paths she herself designated. A fabulous animal fantasy unfolding in every available space, rows of beings and beasts that looked more like an eighteenth-century delirium tremens in color than a comic strip.

Roberta discovered the continuity of the bestiary at the very moment of lifting the cover of the toilet, modestly lowered like an eyelid during sleep that allows its dream to show through.

171

The imagery unfolded in collages of figures clipped from old books avid as traps. Birds and animals from present and past geological eras, interwoven, narrated an ongoing story, spreading over the inside of the cover as well as on the other cover— the oval-shaped ring encircling the whirlpool.

And there were tiny lizards, saurians slithering toward the underside of the ring, allowing the male of the featherless biped species access to the secret zoomorphs during the simple act of urination.

Concatenated images, a kind of loo Rosetta stone, possibly decipherable.

A bathroom to be perused—the last thing Roberta wanted to do at that moment. She turned off the light again and, groping around, sat down on paper feathers and scales that had been diligently shellacked.

There was no distracting oneself with swarming cutouts. The thing to do was to recapture the words from the time when she was writing with the body without even knowing it, let alone having set out to do so:

She had been living in New York for two years or less and thought she knew all the secrets of alley hopping alone at night. Very late on a summer night she'd stepped off the bus on Third Avenue and Eighth Street and straight into the scene: Two characters with identical dark skin and identical wide-brimmed hats, one in a blue satin shirt, the other in a gold one, were quarreling and screaming at one another. The blue one leaned against the blue mailbox, sobbing and shouting his grief at the other, who returned shouts of intermingled hatred and love. Roberta liked the scene, and crossed into it like someone crossing into the stage, and realized that at last she had become part of the theater simply by walking around this terrifying, vital city. The separation between actors and spectators was eliminated, she realized, because the mere fact of walking the streets means we are gambling with our life. She felt proud of herself, and brave: the greatest of prides. With a sense of having grown in stature, of being part of the city like someone walking a tightrope without a safety net below, she left Third Avenue and turned into Stuy-vesant Street, with its gaslight streetlamps, relics of a hundred years ago. (All this she sees rapidly, with her eyes shut, a rec-ollection made of images.) She does not walk fast, feels happy, self-congratulatory, levitating on that tightrope of a city sidewalk that is sheer theater.

The flash that had struck her then recurs now, as she sits on the toilet in the dark. Because against her body there appears (appeared) a man's shadow. Just as she is turning around, it dawns on her that when you enter a scene you cannot allow yourself to be distracted for a single moment. This man is not beside her, but about two yards away, and he says, Don't be afraid, I won't hurt you. If I had wanted to do something, you can be sure I would have been very careful not to cast my shadow.

In the darkness of the bathroom, there are no threatening shad-ows. Or there are, in Roberta, aware of how hard it will be for her to be at one again with the brightest aspects of the city—little figures cut out of all the books of fables in the world.

Perfect gentlemen, Agustín and the critic were waiting for her at the door. I'd like to tell you what we're about to see upstairs, said the critic to Roberta without a trace of suspense, deepening Agustín's anxiety but arousing his curiosity. I want to tell both of you for as novelists you'll appreciate it in its full splendor— about a work of love, as you'll soon see—and prepare yourselves for any surprise because old Edouard can't move but he always has something up his sleeve for us. He was a disciple of Diaghilev, I'm told, a friend of Nijinsky, I'm told—and watch the other two carefully, the old man's protégés, Mark and Antoine, catch the names. As you'll see, the boys are capable of anything for the sake of amusing the venerable old man. In the course of time they invented a world for him, a theater, and sometimes the old man will consent to perform his own version of *Mon ami Pierrot*, which, hopefully, we'll be spared, for it can be both moving and miserable.

The three of them, during the laborious ascent of the freight elevator, are seated on the black velvet bench watching the enormous gears and wheels of the roof draw closer as Lara operates the counterweight. The critic brings them up to date, describing to the two somewhat fearful novelists, huddled a bit too closely together, the transformations of the top-floor loft, which began as a dance studio where Edouard lived and gave classes until his favorite pupil, the Frenchman Antoine, moved in with him and built the mezzanine with an imposing staircase and balconies. And the years went by, and Antoine was no longer seventeen but thirty and the old man ailing, the young man began bringing lovers to the loft, young boys he found when cruising at night, and the old man sat behind a translucent wall, another theatrical device, or behind a one-way mirror, though he preferred the translucent wall because that allowed him to hear and be heard, he could approve or disapprove, accepting the lover and letting things go their natural, or unnatural, course, though they insist it is nature's only true one, or disapproving at the top of his lungs, waving his cane, in which case the transient lover had to be quickly dislodged and rushed off, whether it was the middle of the night or early dawn, cold or hot outside, under the harshest wintry gale if such was the case, and an acceptable replacement found. And so life went on in that agitated way, the critic went on, with only occasional dance classes and demonstrations by pupils who had lost the discipline of the past, until Mark appeared on the scene. On one of those nights on the town, with Antoine going from bar to bar enjoying the goodies to be had in the rear quarters—his own and those of the bar, of course—making the most of it since no one potentially acceptable to Edouard appeared, though for him they would do—any guy was acceptable providing certain attributes were available, transient to be sure, but absolute anonymity was what you were after and watch out if words were exchanged, pleasantries or stuff like that, for those were other times, with never any mention of dangers beyond the imminent, understandable, and even desirable dangers, dangers you were looking for because that after all is what it's all about, life is full of dangers anyway—so, as I was saying, on a night of carousing in shady corners, with little benefit as far as Edouard was concerned, Mark appeared, not in a back room but simply walking along the street, and it seems that Antoine approached him, though now they'll tell you that it was a magical encounter, made for each other, things like that, and he brought him home and collapsed on the mattress that was clearly prepared for other activities in the middle of the large dance studio, facing the barre and mirrors but particularly Edouard's transparent wall, behind which he was waiting impatiently or possibly had already fallen asleep—that never came out—and Antoine remained sound asleep out of sheer exhaustion and Edouard expressed no disapproval or anything, and so Mark stayed on with them and gradually changed their landscape.

Until it wound up years later as you will see it when the floodgates open
to reveal the depths of the mother cave
the dense velvety blackness of the great theatre of the world
the unveiling of that which never did, never should have, never will come to light
the other mask of fantasy,

which in Lara's living space tended toward the perverse, childish smile: the dark side of the moon, the face never visible until this dazzling moment
accompanied by
the creaking of the heavy doors of the freight elevator gliding over the runners

but not so much:

just another face of the human imagination, revealing what is vaguely scary and discomfiting.

It was the grand, impressive private theater that the two boys had rigged up with maternal patience for the diversion of the great maestro, to distract him from his decrepitude and arthritis.

Lara's other guests were already seated in assorted chairs, waiting for something to happen. A completely secret, inner spectacle, because the old man, hidden behind the screen in his huge bed amid patchwork quilts and Persian cushions, was refusing to show himself. Please, *Mon ami Pierrot*, begged the boys who were no longer so boyish, unable to hide their wrinkles even with makeup and dim lighting. *Mon ami Pierrot*, please, they begged not for the pleasure of hearing him sing but because they knew that was the only way of keeping him alive. But the old man refused without refusing, not even blinking an eye or raising a finger. What's to become of us? sighed the boys contritely at the head of the old man's bed.

Your wrinkles will vanish, you will dance again, you'll perform the extravagant dances choreographed by Edouard, a genius in his day, but even a genius can't be expected to be a genius forever, let him simply cease to be one, and live on, intoned Glenn from the other side of the screen, seated in the audience waiting for a show that would not go on.

"I don't know what they want from that poor old man there in bed—enough that he's here with us at all," somebody said.

"In his mobile casket," added the critic.

Glenn cast him a withering look. The critic, insensitive, persisted.

"Yes, as though laid out in that vertical mobile casket that the boys" ("a labor of love," Glenn was saying) "that the boys built to give him an illusion of performing just by sitting there, mouthing the words of *Mon ami Pierrot*, pretending to be singing while flourishing or waving a limp, half-wilted rose, and all of us applauding."

"It was sublime," Glenn went on, ignoring the other speaker. "Because it was an act of love: the boys wheeled the booth from one spot on the stage to another, the lighting inside the stall or kiosk or box office or whatever changing and giving a sensation of movement."

"With the static old man barely whispering," concluded the critic, who wanted the real thing and not just beautiful, pathetic intimations, thought Roberta, and there you have true theater, also known as life, thought Roberta, and felt an impulse to caress Agustín but restrained it.

The boys meanwhile had ceased propping Edouard up but did not want him to lose his audience. They emerged from the mystery zone onto the emptiness of the stage and began inviting the kind assemblage to enter in threes, for the sleeping cubicle qua mausoleum had room for no more than that, with its profusion of kilims and tapestry-covered cushions and incunabula and lamps with beaded shades.

Almost no one looked at Edouard's face, or even checked whether his eyes were open. For protruding from the edge of the mountain of quilts, where his long legs ended, were the old man's slender, perfect feet, the young feet of a dancer, his nails painted dark blue and flecked with white specks.

The boys will do anything to distract the old man, the critic would later insist. And Roberta was left with that single image of Edouard as a huge toy.

By the light of a neon moon suspended overhead, the great ballet master, friend of my friend Pierrot, had shut his eyes to sleep or possibly to die, full of respect for his own symptoms, responding to the rumors about him and his last agony. Agustín had taken advantage of the lull to seek refuge in a remote corner of the loft theater, in the hope of meeting the same fate as the old man. He wished he could go just like that, without a peep, vanishing from this world. To expire, that's what he wanted, to exhale one last sigh: a link to the breath of life, a letting oneself go to the other side.

The setting was right. Wooden beams that had once known paint, now peeling like the peeling walls covered with old curtains to hide or highlight the deterioration. And far away in that room, the one with the translucent screens, Edouard dying or at some point having died while his once young pupils, quite deteriorated themselves, were dancing in close embrace before the enormous baroque-framed mirror that duplicated the already vast expanse, that duplicated the embracing couple and the surrounding images of the home theater but did not reflect Roberta at the other end of the loft. Roberta in animated conversation with several strangers as if Agustín no longer existed in her life, as if the shadow of a murdered woman were dispelled, as if the victim had not been Roberta, too, in part.

Agutín pressed his eyelids until he saw lights. Roberta the dead woman, he repeated to himself in confusion, and what about Edwina?

Edwina had been the name of the dead woman and now he

was mixing it up with Roberta's name. Names, bodies: all mixed up. NN, no name, nonsense. Please, no, please. In his confusion the much sought-after answer could not be found, and yet he felt a little closer to the answer. Or to erasure.

Sometimes by killing the other one tries to kill a mark, a symbol. That's no reason for becoming a murderer, no reason to kill with an actual death.

Sometimes one might have to kill that part of oneself so prone to causing death.

Without necessarily getting entangled in reality as sticky as a spiderweb.

To kill without killing, by killing. The phrase took him by surprise, catapulted him to his feet, as if to flee from himself or to tear himself from his own skin. Drained, he stared with infinite astonishment as the cushions that retained the form of his body. I carry the form of my body with me, he said to himself, and felt alien to that idea emerging from his innermost secret labyrinths.

He felt the need then to escape that physical space, carrying with him his entire skin and body and his labyrinths. But to achieve that he would have to cross the entire desolate pampas that was once a stage in a theater, walk past Roberta and give her some explanation, say goodbye, and then, then—get into that awful freight elevator he didn't know how to operate, sit down by himself on the ridiculous velvet-covered bench, pull the chain in a ridiculous imitation of a giant toilet. In his childhood the toilet was called the throne. Precisely. And seated on that throne of disaster, he'd be forced to pull the chain to hurtle to the bottom of the abyss where he rightly belonged.

That's it. Enough negative self-portraits. The main thing was to face Roberta and tell her he was leaving, he was splitting this scene.

Agustín could see Roberta on the other side, where the stage would be if there were a real stage, beyond this penumbra, standing in a distant penumbra of a different tone. A patch of white approached her, embraced her, and Agustín realized that the patch was Bill just arriving, or rather, Bill's sweater, for Bill himself is decidedly not white.

Then he could not get over there. His way out had been blocked. Seized from him, assuming that the way out was or might pass by Roberta.

The way out, he instructed himself, was not to be found in others but in groping through one's own penumbra and finding a new opening. It lay in one's own imagination, in the page that was blank only a moment ago. Where was it not? It was not in the woman who knew only how to go around in circles, nor in the descending freight elevator, nor in fear of oneself, nor—

It was in moving ahead on one's own legs, in groping one's way along walls, because now he heard something that sounded like familiar, soothing music coming from the other side.

Behind a drape he discovered what he was looking for without knowing it: a passage to other latitudes. Since nothing could surprise him anymore, since he was following a trail of sound, he simply had to separate the drapes, cross an opening without a door, and go down a few steps to find himself in a well-lit, white-walled living room with plants, pale furniture, and other elements of normal living.

"Hello," said a man sprawled in an armchair strumming a

guitar. "Hello. Not many people venture down here from the heights."

"Not very lofty heights, just five steps," Agustín replied without realizing that he was being addressed in his own language.

"Don't you believe that. Those are Olympian heights, Parnassus or something, a temple."

"A mausoleum."

"That too. And I'm the caretaker. Because of Edouard, the sacred old man. I'm the only one he allows to look after him. Which explains the five steps. This is another building, but we opened up the partition."

"He's dying."

"Yes. He's been dying for a long time. When the disease grabs old people, degeneration is very slow but relentless."

"The same with everyone."

"The same with everything."

And the man went back to his guitar.

Agustín thought he had been forgotten until he began to recognize the melody, felt it getting to him. Moved, he said, "It's a *triste pampeano*."

"Right. For a sad man from the pampas."

So many things can be learned across walls, from one building to another, thought Agustín.

"Help yourself to a drink. There on the table. Take whatever you want—the ice is on the left. And no, I wasn't expecting you, don't look at me like that, but when there's a performance on the other side someone always drops in. Some more literally than others—sometimes a person flops down the steps and then he really needs a drink to get him out of shock. I may be a doctor but I don't discount home remedies, quite the opposite. I'm a Uruguayan, lived for many years in Buenos Aires, when it was our turn to seek refuge on the other side of the puddle, and you have such a *porteño* look to you it kills me. To answer your unspoken question. So just have a seat—you look as if you need a chair and a drink and maybe a good chat."

Agustín sat down with a glass in his hand and a clear awareness of what he was doing: escaping Roberta, who to his horror or grief was no longer pursuing him, if indeed she ever had.

We haven't introduced ourselves, the guitar player says between chords. I'm Hector Bravo—plunk, plunk—say he and his guitar. I'm a doctor—plunkety plunk. Glad to meet you.

And since all the tangos he comes up with just to keep strumming the instrument seem like an ironic commentary on his words, he lays aside the guitar and waits. Waits for the visitor to say, And my name is such and such, and for a friendly, inconsequential conversation to ensue. The visitor remains silent, the host says to himself, Hmm, another one with problems— and since the problems of others are his specialty and true vocation—the guitar being merely a hobby—and since at half past two in the morning one can expect very few surprises if one has chosen to remain on house call, he starts throwing out cues to make the visitor loosen up and eventually pour out his story.

Hector Bravo rests his legs on the glass of the rattan table, stretches, crosses his arms behind his head in a characteristic pose, and starts talking as if thinking aloud.

"When we made that opening to the other loft, absolutely illegal, you understand, I wanted it to be like a passageway, a birth canal. You know, like coming out of the shadows into the light, from darkness to brightness—and I tried hard to make everything here as bright as possible. But the others overpowered me, as you see, and hung those horrible, hairy curtains, and since I'm the one who uses the passage most, every time I go to see the old man I have to wedge through the hairs, losing all sense of poetry and winding up in cobwebs of darkness. Harsh reality, you might say. Only it isn't reality at all, but a bad imitation. You must have realized this at first glance: Opaque surfaces are transparent, mirrors allow you to see through them, the heavy rocks on the stairway—if you can call it that—leading to Antoine's room are painted papier-mâché, the puppets are alive and the men less so, the black cat is simply a projection, slides that flash now and then, against a false window or on a shelf, so that the old man may think his cat Amletto is still alive, or at least is coming to visit him as ectoplasm. Nothing is what it appears to be, and whenever I climb those puny steps I feel as if I were being born in reverse and often tell myself that that after all *is* reality. True, harsh, deceptive, gripping, fluctuating, imaginative, exciting, damned reality. Your humble servant."

And so began a game of transitive fascinations:

Dr. Bravo fascinated by Edouard's illness and his slow agony; Agustín Palant, despite his bucking, fascinated now by Hector Bravo. A feeling that gradually permeated him through those hours they spent together waiting for something difficult to define.

Slowly Agustín began to recover a long-forgotten calm, and that nightly vigil of the other, not centered on his own anxiety, did something to restore his confidence in his fellowman. He dozed now and then, rose now and then to pour himself another drink, listened now and then; Hector's words, Hector's guitar, Hector's cassettes. He felt a strange sense of brotherliness, a gradual return to the world of humans, of men perhaps, to a place where violence has a well-designated, orderly function.

He thought or dreamed of a surgeon's scalpel. Thought or dreamed of precise geometric forms. Thought or dreamed or perhaps glimpsed through lowered lids the emerging light of daybreak. He dreamed of white, white walls, a glaring light striking his eyes. It wasn't an operating room, no. He woke up, startled, perspiring. A nightmare, he explained to Hector, then added: "Like an interrogation."

"You had too much to drink."

"Sorry."

"What's to be sorry about? It's sometimes therapeutic. Talking is also good, if you'd like to."

"Some other time. I can't now. I have to go back next door, across the wall. They're waiting for me and must be worried."

"You're the one who's worried. The wall is closed again, don't you see? The passage is a nocturnal one. There's a library now where the curtains were, and no more guests left on the other side. The old man is sleeping, you mustn't disturb him now. Let's get some sleep ourselves. The wake is over. You can stretch out on this couch. Here's a blanket. And then you'll see."

"I have to leave word."

"What for? They know you're with me. Everyone knows about the passageway, it's no secret. You won't have vanished, right?"

"Being a one-patient doctor is a strange fate. But I'm not complaining. It's useful for my research, and besides, I'm afraid that at some point, in two, three, five years—the incubation time is very long—I'll have two other patients next door. Or more. They usually bring their friends and some stay on for a while, like one guy named Jack whom we've now lost. But that's not my motive. I never got my license here and can't practice legally, hence my long sleepless nights with Edouard. I feel as if I'm back in the hospital, on night duty. You'll be hearing lots of things about me. Some nastier than others. Some really nasty. Don't believe them. At least, don't believe all of them. Here, let me fix your pillow. I'll bring you another blanket in case you feel cold. Tomorrow—that is to say, tonight—is another day."

At seven in the evening they had what they found amusing to call breakfast, and laughed quite a lot. Agustín, with a clearer head, discovered that Hector Bravo was much older than he had supposed the night before. He had taken him for a man his own age or younger, but now he realized that the youthfulness was deceptive. A wrinkled neck, his hands, gave Hector away. All the rest of him looked under forty. Could he be twenty years older? The idea produced an odd mixture of confusion and relief.

"You're much older—" he started to say.

"Oh yes. Farther past my majority than you think. A lieutenant colonel, almost."

Exactly the kind of remark to alarm Agustín, only this time

he could take it as a bad joke. With a lame smile he changed the subject.

"I have to call Roberta."

"Your wife? Your better half, your worse-than-nothing, your beloved?"

"My friend. My pitiless and at times harsh friend."

"Not to be disparaged, man."

"He told me he was with someone by the name of Hector Bravo and now I'm more worried than before."

"Let go. You must learn to cut the umbilical cord, let him get away from you. Hector Bravo. Well. You hear all sorts of things about him."

"Magoo was bound to run into him."

"That wasn't hard. He lives in the loft next to Ed's. They're connected and are like the two faces of a coin. Come on. Don't get upset. Let the guy do what he pleases and you come with me, we'll all be better off."

"I'm so upset, so furious I could die."

"Cut the crap and sit still. I want to get that left eye. Don't tell me. You've got one eye different from the other—let me get your portrait right."

"You promised me a spiritual portrait. What's with all this realism?"

"I like looking at you, and the eye is the most spiritual part of you—the left eye, that is. And I can tell you that your Magoo—"

"Our Magoo."

"Since when? Let's say that Magoo is in good hands. Very good hands. In any case, excellent for him. How shall I put it? A very contradictory character, this Hector Bravo, if that's his name and not an alias."

"You mean pseudonym."

"I mean alias, given the circumstances. A contradictory character, or maybe not. What's contradictory is his reputation. Whatever. Some say one thing about him, others something else.

Others like Antoine say one thing or another according to the way the wind blows. And Dr. Bravo contradicts no one, makes no attempt to clarify or rectify. This lends him a certain solidity, and what your, excuse me, what Magoo needs is solidity. If I'm not mistaken—and don't stand up, keep still, even if it's only a little longer, so I can catch that angle of the nose, just like that, a little more profile, that's it, the shadow's shifting. Hector Bravo, it seems, was a Tupamaro, or a doctor or surgeon for the Tupas. And he helped many of them escape from a military hospital where they were in custody. A great, brave surgeon, that's the bright legend. Because the dark legend also contains a surgical knife, a flayer. Stay just like that for a moment. I feel like kissing you, in that pose."

Roberta smiled faintly, out of sheer weariness. And since Bill hadn't seen a trace of a smile for a long while, he put aside his sketch pad, rose from the floor where he was seated, and lay down on the sofa next to Roberta, his head resting on her knees.

"The dark legend is better told with our arms around each other. Antoine himself told it to me in his darkest moments— he tells it with relish, which makes it more unlikely. I don't believe it. I think that if anything, he was a Tupa. Or maybe he was nothing, which would be the simplest. An ordinary Uruguayan doctor without the credentials to practice here. Edouard's personal, secret physician, involved now in AIDS research, which ennobles him. Or maybe not. Let's see, take your arm away, let me turn around, like this, put your head here— that's good."

"No. Tell me more about the bad reputation."

"Not bad at all. This has a great reputation. Sublime."

"You asshole. Bravo's bad rep."

"Oh, that. I'll tell you some other time. Right now I have other plans."

"Men are all alike, aren't you?"

"Keep still, woman, don't get up, you'll dump me on the floor."

"All you care about is keeping me still. The portrait, your

head here, you won't tell me today but maybe tomorrow. Okay. I have no reason to fight with you. What I want is to fight everyone."

"It's almost Christmas, Rob. Peace on earth, that's what's needed."

"Your grandmother, as we say down south, peace on earth! Magoo and I got into a tough battle and I at least will see it through even if it's not my own battle."

"But what are you fighting for?"

"For knowledge. To know, *tout court*. And it's something so personal for Magoo, perhaps nonexistent, that I'm afraid it's only a defensive battle. I have to defend him from himself."

"If only, if only, if only we could defend one another. Considering how hard it already is to defend oneself. But I recommend that you defend yourself, Bobbie, fight for yourself, get out of this farce. Come back, Roberta, come back, we forgive you."

Hector knows how to listen. Bravo.

Caught up in words that have a place and time of their own, Agustín Palant releases his story. He neither spins nor embroiders it, allowing it to flow like water from a spring, pure in the sense of being uncontaminated by self-censorship, self-pity, fear or sadness.

Hector Bravo doesn't intrude on Agustín's story, merely indicates with a slight exclamation or a nod that he's listening attentively. He breathes with audible effort and the whole house seems to breathe along with him, as though the air were in suspense.

Occasional sighs emanate from the walls but Agustín fails to hear them, or at least pays no attention to them although there are intermittent breaks—syncopated breaks—in the rhythm of his narrative.

Agustín and Hector, meeting now at either end of the narrative, cross Tompkins Square together, emboldened with gun in pocket (the embarrassment of its purchase now over, only the sense of power remaining). They walk along ignoring approaches. It wasn't panhandlers approaching them, then, as they might be today if they crossed that same park. Now hands might be extended with paper cups begging for a handout; then there were claws selling, imposing, or giving away (a theater ticket) to take possession of the waylaid soul.

The breathing—Hector Bravo, Agustín, the walls—is like a

presence punctuating the tale. At times the pauses are prolonged and Hector listens, listens to all the vibrations of the house, hears what is said and what is not said: the word Agustín is groping for through this barely perceptible breathing which resumes a normal rhythm as Agustín recovers his voice to describe his misgivings on entering the theater, that enormous warehouse.

He tells about the soup, recapturing its flavor as well as its bad aftertaste. (That soup repeats on you, Roberta might have said under less adverse circumstances.)

Agustín tells of his eagerness, his need, as he says, to see the actress/cook again that night and to escort her home. His prowling around the theater—and that place has also been lost, for he doesn't know where the theater or its surroundings are—to approach her (to kill her, at that point? He thinks of it as a likely fate. Does not tell Hector that).

There is a slight hiatus, a pause, in the ambient breathing, which Agustín confuses with his own. In order to catch his breath he comes out with the name Edwina. Not meaning to, after such a long time. And that's all he remembers.

I killed her, he adds from that haze of amnesia where not remembering constitutes an intense unity of memory that condenses at the very moment hand thrusts into pocket and draws out revolver.

For the first time, Agustín was able to tell everything without fear of hurting any feelings, and, what's more, of hurting himself. Let this Hector Bravo do as he pleased with the information. As far as he, Agustín Palant, was concerned, he had turned himself in simply by telling his story. What happened afterward didn't matter to him.

He didn't fear betrayal or denunciation, he had only one concern: that this person who had listened with such damn calm might doubt the information.

"You don't believe me. Don't you believe I told you the truth just now?"

"Of course I believe you. Maybe not on the same level you want to be believed, but naturally I believe you. Deeply. A dying man claims to see a white light (and many do see it) and I believe him. Others claim to see angels and I believe them. I believe them when they see rows of animals or hear bells."

"Yeah. But there are no such lights or angels. And those people are dying. I, on the other hand, killed. Do you understand? I killed."

"Don't go asking me to act as judge, or executioner. Not anymore. I told you I'm a doctor: I only know how to cure, whenever possible."

"I killed without even thinking it could happen, that I was going to kill. I killed without understanding why or realizing anything."

"All right then, we'll see, maybe I can help you. To understand. Simply that. Meanwhile, have a drink: while one is alive, it is good to enjoy life."

Because there are some who won't be able to enjoy it anymore, Agustín thought, jumping to his feet, suddenly aware of another sound. The breathing of the walls had given way to a gasping, a rattle. Only then did he detect it, separating it from himself.

"What's that?" he almost shouted.

"Weren't you aware of it? It's the sacred old man, in his death agony. Don't you hear it? I installed a sound monitor in his room. From here I can pick up his faintest call, his sighs. That's his way of calling me now. I'm afraid the moment has come."

He reached for his doctor's satchel.

"You're leaving."

"Yes, I have to attend to the sublime old man. But don't worry, I'll be coming back at some point. Stay here, make yourself at home, settle in—you know where the blankets are—raid the refrigerator, what little there is. It's going to be a long night. I'll think about what you told me, if I'm given time to think. I'm afraid that—anyhow, don't worry. We'll do something, and remember, as long as we're alive we're all immortal, as somebody once said.

And off he ran toward the sound of the gasps, disappearing in the short passageway through which Agustín had burst into his loft the night before.

Bill was again summoning Roberta back but she had finally succeeded in convincing him that in order to return you must first leave. A return voyage requires that you complete the outgoing journey, whatever it may be, and if possible bring something back with you. Some element with which to wipe the slate clean. Clean slate, new story, turn the page. Easy to say. Turn the corner for now, and the corner of time, and walk and cross a boundary once again and press a certain bell next to an indistinct nameplate that explains nothing. Where You Know is the name Roberta finally has given the place, because everything there is so foreseen and predictable.

Roberta has gone to get a manuscript, not her own, and she's gone alone. Bill had insisted on accompanying her but was dissuaded. What if he took the place seriously? What if he had a notion to judge her, to question her right to stick herself into worlds such as this, which she enters solely as the novelist she is, a mere mystifier?

Agustín had phoned again, this time to tell her not to worry about him—as though she had been worrying, as though he knew she'd been worrying—that he was staying at Hector Bravo's place because apparently old Edouard was breathing his last—as if the old man were a close relative, though they'd barely caught a glimpse of him in his high bed. Yet something in all of that had driven her into the wintry streets at night and led her to this very door in search of some papers.

• • •

The downstairs buzzer rings. Roberta is relieved: maybe she's been recognized on the monitor. She pushes the door open and climbs the steps. On the second floor she finds herself face-to-face with the fat woman at her very bureaucratic desk, and is spared questions or filling out a form because the fat one recognizes her as Ava Taurel's writer friend who has landed here on another occasion in awful oxfords that shatter the atmosphere of spike heels and high black boots, and this time it's brown rain boots—how perverse.

Roberta explains to Baby Jane—knowing she's called Baby Jane because Agustín couldn't resist telling her—that she's coming for her friend's manuscripts, which she herself left here, and to please call Ava, since she's in a bit of a hurry.

"I'll tell you just what I told that cutie pie when he came: If you want the folders, you'll have to find them. It's like a treasure hunt. Just go ahead and look. That's the rule."

"Rule? What rule? I only want to get my friend's manuscripts back. I brought them here for safekeeping and now I've got to return them. That's all."

"Oh no. Everything here is very orderly. Regimented. Things are as we stipulate. If you're looking for anarchy and out to have your own sweet way, you should've gone to a whorehouse to hide your precious papers."

And so Roberta starts the search, opening the doors of cubicles with a bit of disgust and also a measure of curiosity and fear.

Doors are opened and shut almost immediately, for Magoo's manuscripts can not be found there. What is found there is the notorious cage close to the ceiling, and stocks, some occupied by naked supplicants apparently begging for more.

A blindfolded man appears behind the door of one of the cubicles, his nipples pierced with rings. Two dominatrices are preparing him and seem about to suspend him from the rings. Roberta stands riveted by the scene until she hears a laugh behind her. It is Ava, tearing her from her contemplation and her unspoken question: What do onlookers like myself make of scenes like this, what do they feel, imagine, or fantasize?

"Laugh," Ava prompts her. "The guy can't see us, and it's good for him to believe that we're here in force, that we're powerful and are laughing at him."

"I have no power and don't want any," Roberta replies, closing yet another door, shutting off another scene. "All I want are Agustín's things. And also a piece of info: Do you know someone by the name of Hector Bravo? It seems he was a torturer."

"Hector Bravo—forget it. He's only a vampire of death. A student of death, he claims. Listen, if he'd been a torturer, he'd be working for us by now, we would have put him back in business."

And she spins around with willow rod in hand, going off to resume her interrupted duties.

Baby Jane's expression or perhaps her enormous breasts prompt Roberta to open yet another door, the last one she'll have the courage, she thinks, to face. All she's looking for are some written pages and not a sampler of human desolation.

She would like to just stand still in that long corridor full of closed doors like the corridor of a convalescent home, a psychiatric hospital, Steppenwolf's magic theater. To stand and wait for some terrifying illumination. But she knows that she must take another step—there's always one more step to take when one believes the limit has been reached—and she opens an apparently innocuous door, behind which people talk not about their own desire but about the mauled desire of others.

What she finds there might have conveyed a certain air of innocence were it not where it was. A boudoir with women's lingerie, a sofa draped in fox skins, feather boas hanging on a bentwood rack.

Roberta resolves to enter, takes a few steps, opens (not without certain apprehension, wishing momentarily for a pair of those aggressive yellow rubber gloves with which the police express their revulsion and fear at sticking their hands into certain—

human—masses) the top drawer of the bureau, opens the second drawer under the prompting of Baby Jane's eyes, rummages among lace bras and possibly contaminated bikinis worn or to be worn by the masculine clientele of the establishment, and finally finds what she was looking for.

"Good nose," Baby Jane tells her. "That cutie pie was here a long time, right on this sofa, and didn't find a thing. I wonder why."

With Agustín's folders inside her handbag, the fleece-lined raincoat over her shoulders, Roberta wants to run away. She takes the wrong door. Enough of wrong doors, always getting into places where she doesn't belong or that are least suitable. Though sometimes she doesn't get into them herself. Sometimes she is pushed, and maybe once again Baby Jane contrived this displacement or immersion into forbidden regions.

Suddenly Roberta finds herself not at the exit but facing a small stage. There is no one in the audience, but on the stage is a big vertical wooden wheel, a medieval torture instrument, with a half-naked woman tied to its spokes, her arms and legs apart as in Leonardo's famous illustration of harmonious proportion. It is not harmony that the woman depicts but expectation of something terrifying and presumably delicious. A man is officiating. Bare-chested, wearing black leather trousers and wristlets studded with spikes. A classic outfit. With classic gaze he regards the woman who waits tied to the wheel. Suddenly he sets it spinning, wheel with bound woman, and the woman lets out a scream, head down. The man returns her to her previous position, just for a few moments, and again, with an indifferent expression, spins the wheel. Woman head down, blood rushing to her head to the bursting point. The man lashes her with a whip and then consoles her. He licks her crotch at the golden center of her being, right next to the ring piercing the lips of her vulva.

• • •

Turn around, Roberta. Turn again, march. She can't. Baby Jane as usual is, with her entire bulk, blocking her escape.

"Why do people kill?" Roberta asks as a gambit to get past her.

Baby Jane has only one reply.

"For pleasure."

"Pleasure in killing? Is there pleasure in killing?"

"For the pleasure of being killed by the other."

8

Hey. Thanks for waiting up, it's nice sometimes to have someone waiting for you. And thanks for the coffee—right now I think I'd prefer a scotch. It's over there, lift that lid. I told you to make yourself at home, you could have gone to sleep on the daybed, like last night, but I'm glad to find you awake. It's all over. Add more ice, please. I did what I could, and luckily was there to lend a hand, one way or another. We were waiting for the moment; they left me alone with him and I managed to remind him that the death of a man like himself who has lived his life fully has to be joyful. A man who's known how to occupy all of his place so completely, fill it with his body and stretch his body to the maximum, make his body reach all the corners like the dancer and choreographer he was, cannot die shrunken and shriveled. A man as great as he, a sublime old man, must take full command of space. Imagine at this very moment, I told him, on how many stages of the world your dances are being performed. And now you, too, are going to dance in all those ballets, on all, all, all the stages of this world and of the other. Each one of your particles is going to dance, all your infinite atoms will dance throughout infinite eternity: that is true glory. You will be present in every *Rite of Spring* that's danced, your choreography by now is classic, and you with it. I felt very inspired at that moment, truly the old man's great moment, and told him, Not to mention *Coppelia,* and he said, No, for God's sake, let's not mention *Coppelia.* I'm fed up with *Coppelia,* we're living among dolls. And he burst out laughing. I joined his laughter as best I could. Laughter is ideal for dying, though few achieve it. And he kept laughing at the thought of Ratcliff's puppets, his numerous, varied, huge puppets, and Rat's sad fate, adopted son of a madwoman collector, raised to be the world's greatest puppeteer. Imagine—when he was only five, she started filling the house with Sicilian puppets, the most extensive collection in the world, nineteenth-century puppets, and then brought the greatest maestro from Palermo to teach him how to manipulate them. With tiny puppets at times and sometimes with puppets larger than Rat himself, the maestro taught him to perform Orlando Furioso, pulling the strings from above the stage, Orlando Furioso over and over, he powerless to express his own rage, the master making him work the strings of puppets that kept growing and usurping the kid's place, imagine that, Edouard said with a bare thread of a voice now as if gently tugging on another puppet. Just imagine the poor bastard, said the old man who anyway was the son of some obscure Russian prince of lowly lineage. And the kid, the only benefit he got from moving his hands so deftly was for a good jerk-off, let me tell you, up and down, up and down. The old man was laughing and panting, and I was thinking of the other two guys who looked after him and where they'd gone off to, and better they weren't there, they would only have started crying and messing things up and the old man needed that laughter, the drifting into someone else's story that was using up the little breath he had left. Then suddenly he broke off and with the same tears of laughter said, I'm a pathetic figure. Why do they make me do this old-fogy number? It's shameful. *Mon ami Pierrot*, pathetic. Not really, I told him, it's pathetic and beautiful at the same time. Forget the pathetic part and remember just the beautiful; you're a traveler now and must travel light. Carry along with you only the beautiful, the joyous. This is going to be your great trip, and remember, when someone sets out on a trip, he wants to organize everything at the last moment and gets all snarled up and confused and sticks his foot into the wrong places and does foolish things. But when the plane rises, everything falls into place: what didn't get done no longer matters, shame is gone, and also the mistakes. All of that gets left behind in the other country. One takes along only what is good and the good memories.

After a while he asked me to step inside the contraption the boys had rigged up for him to do his show. The simulator of movement. He asked me to turn on the colored strobes and although luckily no one was there to jostle me, I still felt like a ticket seller in a box office. The ticket seller of death—dig the fine irony—and I got out of it as soon as I could and said to him, Look, we're all pathetic, that's what makes us more human. Death also humanizes us, I told him with great effort, my task not being an easy one, and I realized at that moment how much I loved the old man. I went over and embraced him. He was a lovable human being in all his poetic perversion and his genius. I didn't want him to slip away from me. I held him with all my strength and then released him. I could no longer bring him back; I had to help him go. I'd been preparing for that all these months, years perhaps, years with other people and now the lovable old man. Recognition of our own death is our most human endowment, I wanted to tell him, but now he could barely hear me. He made me bend over very close to his face, once more, and asked, as I felt him slipping away, Sing "Au clair," and I with my awful voice—what little was left of it at that moment—took the plunge and began, Au clair de la lune/ mon ami Pierrot/ prête moi ta plume/ pour écrire un mot ... With his hand he made a weak ritornello gesture, and I began all over—about five or six times I began again. It was a kind of litany, a lullaby. A scratched record. I would have gone on forever but the old man squeezed my hand gently and I stopped in time to hear him say,

What could be the word that he wants

and he kept me in suspense. Only after a very long silence did he add, or sigh

... to write?

And that was it.

Where You Know, Roberta keeps repeating along the snow-covered streets, trying to tread cautiously, so as not to slide on the patches of ice. Once she slipped and began falling down ever so slowly. Where You Know, maybe there they know something we don't—she was falling ever so slowly, she couldn't prevent it and landed sprawled out belly up like a cockroach. Maybe at Where You Know they possess the knowledge intuited by Djuna Barnes, that of Little Red Riding Hood in bed with the wolf; maybe they know or suspect or seek the sublime side of pain. Does pain have a sublime side? There she was, hip badly banged, in the snowy, solitary night, not this night but another one, unable to get up on her own, and laughing, laughing. Maybe at Where You Know they're trying to know (but don't), and keep going round and round in circles repeatedly—while she, flat on her back in the street, surrenders, feet apart, mouth open, laughing, unable to control herself. At Where You Know there's a fixed, custom-made ritual; in real pain nothing is custom-made, real pain has no limits. That fall wasn't real pain, dark roach against clean white virgin snow, dark roach, dark solitary street, it was just a hearty laugh at wanting to stand up and not being able to, propping herself on one hand and slipping, unable to stand, trying to get a foothold and slipping, unable to do so. At Where You Know all are able to, all are able, the exact form of their fantasies designed to order: I want my balls wrung, and you get your balls wrung to the limit, as if there were nothing more or even different, as if being alive weren't an ongoing discovery of the unknown dream, the unanticipated desire.

Proceeding along that most untropical of sidewalks, she plants each footstep firmly to break the icy crust. It's not always possible. Where You Know has been left behind. She will not return. Sometimes she still has a faint memory of the pain of that banged hip. One spot as a reminder of the surprise, of the laughter induced by the surprise, and also of the pain. Does the pain remain and the surprise vanish, or vice versa? At Where You Know they're probably unconcerned about such aftereffects. At Where You Know only the staging of that which doesn't—never mind. The snow falls slowly, a caressing of the streets, and people come out with their dogs and celebrate, as though with little bells; tomorrow, Sunday, will be sunny and with luck there won't be any snowplows and then— then they'll be able to pull out their cross-country skis and glide down Fifth Avenue, white and silent and bright and more alive than ever. An easy gliding, as though there were no chance of falling.

Agustín had seemed to be a Where You Know man even though he only set foot there at her bidding. The Witch's Castle, he'd called it then, to play it down, and also the House of Funny Mirrors. He has a name for every threat. He also has certain manuscripts—without a name—which she, Roberta, will have the pleasure of returning to him.

Then on to something else.

That is, if there is still a possibility of healing, of forgetting.

Roberta begins softly whistling the song Edouard never sang for her. For an intense moon is out, and by the light of the moon friend Pierrot is being asked for a pen with which to write *un mot*. That might well be a motto or nickname or an alias or *mot d'esprit* all of them could use. *Esprit*. That is.

Luckily Bill will be waiting for her with some tasty concoction or some other tasty item—the cooked and the raw—which she certainly could use after so much indigestion from heavy, revolting food.

She decides to continue on foot to her cramped dwelling. It's quite a walk, and despite the late hour all sorts of Christmas vendors are offering their wares beneath plastic awnings. Toys, Christmas tree decorations, music boxes, red and green candles, streamers. And in the midst of such cheery placidity, one is selling braided leather whips, long as lizard tails.

Roberta is telling Bill about the street vendors at that hour of the night, and how she felt like buying him a gift. A teddy bear sprinkled with snow that resembled him, but there is not much cash left, so.

"Not to worry, there'll be plenty of opportunities. Meanwhile that critic from the other night phoned to ask you for an erotic short story. It seems they're preparing an anthology. He says it pays well, but I told him that you don't write that kind of stuff. He said to stop kidding, that he'd leafed through a couple of your books and knew the score. Better than I, apparently. He needs something unpublished."

"I've got nothing unpublished. Haven't been writing lately. I'll have to go be a saleswoman in your shop, or find some other job."

"As you wish. I have no special thing for women writers, and it bugs me that critics with playboy pretensions phone soon after meeting them to ask for whatever. And thinking it over, I want you to come with me. Not to sell, to live in my pad. We could fix it up nicely. Here there's no room for another pin; in back of my shop we could rearrange the space, fix it to suit ourselves. You'd be comfortable there, you wouldn't have to write erotic stories on demand."

"Big deal. I've been involved in an erotic story larger than life lately. Just have to put it into words to earn the critic's dough.

So what. Just have to stop writing it with the body, and so vicariously to boot, the body cringing, bristling, scared, anxious to bolt, without the slightest grace."

And sparing no details, she describes to Bill the latest scenes at Where You Know.

"All women? The ones who dominate are all women?"

"Most. At least in that place. To balance things a little, I suppose."

It has grown quite late. But there is still time to describe a memory of the distant night of the party, the one thrown by the elderly bride, which might well be the seed for the requested erotic story.

The guests are saying goodbye, and among those departing is a young, lushly pregnant dominatrix on the arm of her young husband. From the depths of the audience someone shouts out to them: Is the baby going to be dominator or dominated? Dominated, I hope, replies the father-to-be. Then let's pray it's a boy! someone shouts from the depths (of his soul).

(To be dominated is the best, they say, always trying to appropriate what isn't theirs. It's the best, they say. That way we are the incarnation of the other's fantasy. We *are* the fantasy.)

Roberta finishes telling the story, editorializing it, and knows she is never going to be able to write that scene in all its disgusting candor. Lately everything comes to her so mixed together, and writing should be the opposite of cooking: an ability to separate the ingredients so as to understand what the cake is made of, placing the flour here and the butter there and the salt quite far from the sugar and discarding poisons as much as possible.

But that's not writing either with the body or with the pen (lend it to me) nor is it anything; it's merely plunging into entropy. Wishing to run the film backward, to dismount from the world. She thinks of her half-finished novel in a drawer of the filing cabinet. She thinks of that other drawer in her desk where she put unopened letters, maybe one of them inviting her to give a lecture or to write an essay.

"I like your offer of living in the store and forgetting about all those scribbled pages. I have a horrible feeling that I'm never going to write again."

"Not to worry. For all the reading I do."

A rites-of-passage man, Hector Bravo, therefore unable and unwilling to have anything to do with the old man's body. It's the next evening and Mark and Antoine have taken over: they've left in place the bookcases that close off the passageway between the two lofts, as if it were daytime.

"I don't think I'll be belonging to the building next door anymore. That scene is over for me," Hector says.

Agustín as usual wants reasons.

"Those two aren't going to let anyone horn in. I've fulfilled my duties to them, and they'll forget about me. So what. The old man is not there anymore, even if they're sitting vigil a few yards away. They probably have made him up like crazy. They said they'd take charge of preparing the body. I even heard they were going to paint the coffin like a Russian Easter egg. Poor Edouard. They robbed him of all his dignity, but he had fun with them. A good thing. The line has been drawn and I've remained on this bank of the river. It'll be good for me, I admit. The only think I took from next door was Frieda the puppet. I borrowed her for you."

"The puppet? For me? And why not an inflatable doll?"

"You were telling me your story when the Great Interruption took place. Frieda may serve as a link. Keep in mind what Lara says about her. She too is an actress."

"Fuck you," says Agustín, quick on the offensive.

Agustín is ready to slam the door and take off. But just then he realizes that he has nowhere to go, that he doesn't even have his overcoat, which he left on the other side.

He tries to excuse himself: "I don't know where the limit is."

"But there is a limit, and very clearly defined. Pointing it out is the function of us thanatologists—if you'll excuse the expression. What's usually missing is the think you're looking for: a precise explanation. We'll never know exactly how the mechanism works."

"Like Roberta's novel, the novel Roberta tells: Two guys take refuge on the ground floor of a big abandoned house while a murdered woman with her brains popping out is walking around on the second story, holding the ax used in the crime, looking for revenge. And the terrible thing is that we'll never know how the story ends. The book got lost."

"Maybe there is no real ending. Maybe it was an open novel—not a gothic novel, as you both seem to think. I'll repeat an absurd Chinese proverb that Edouard was fond of: 'Never swat a fly on your friend's head with an ax.'"

"Very clear."

"You need an explanation for every single thing. You even wanted to kill a woman in search of an explanation. You blew the lid off her brains to find out what was inside her head."

"I didn't want to kill her. Not that I wanted to. I did. Without any motive, without even realizing it. And to think that up until then I believed I had everything under control, to think that I always distrusted passions."

"You see. Edouard would tell you that there is no possible control. Only passions. He was Russian, it's true; he was also a very wise man. Relax, don't be on the defensive all the time. Kill the pressure of that death in yourself now, and don't feel so omnipotent. 'Yet each man kills the thing he loves,' said the poet."

"Words. I need to understand myself, to understand why I did it. If not I'll go crazy."

"I can give you a slew of reasons, all clever and equally valid:

207

You killed her because you saw in her a mother image you didn't like. An image of all women, of a certain woman in particular, and we're not naming names. You killed her because she made you confront a most unbearable frustration, from way back. Because you wanted to kill in her your own feminine image. See all the things that occur to me, how sharp I am? We're all hung up on sordid, unilluminating motivations. You killed her because you were fed up with facing feminine demands, or your own. That is, assuming you killed her, because we can't be sure. You said it was a point-blank shot, in her temple, didn't you? You would have gotten splattered. I don't know. Maybe not, with a .22. You'd have to ask a ballistics expert. I'm not recommending that, and besides, what difference does it make after all if you really killed her or dreamed it? It's all the same. The same impunity and the same guilt; tell yourself it was self-defense. It happened without your knowing it, in a third state that won't recur. Possibly it was the necessary step to distance yourself from something unbearable in your past."

"Shut up! Let me sleep, I'm dead tired. Stop upsetting me."

"Think of what there was in your past."

"Nothing. Nothing, and that's what's so terrifying, nothing while tenants in my own apartment building in Buenos Aires were being hauled away, with hoods over their heads, and we never saw them again. Nothing, when people came asking for my help and I could do nothing—what do you expect me to have done?—when I didn't even believe them, not even when María Inés—"

"María Inés?"

"It doesn't matter. It doesn't matter what she said to me, I don't even know where she went, or even remember her. I don't know anything, writing is all I know."

"And did you write anything about all this?"

There is a long bridge of silence. Agustín finally crosses over.

"You think that I believe in cathartic writing."

"I do. Here's the typewriter, pay no attention to me. And

there's paper in that drawer over there," Hector Bravo adds, suspecting that it will remain blank.

It was the night that remained a blank for both of them, not the day. Hector's schedule was inverted and Agustín found it contagious. The circadian cycle, he thought, mentally trying to sort out the skein of Hector Bravo's words (words, words), which could only serve as a springboard to something else.

11

"He died, one might say, with his boots on."

"That is, with little stars painted on his toenails."

Roberta was relieved not to have to explain anything to Bill. The best thing about their relationship was their tacit understanding despite language differences.

After living in Bill's domain for a couple of days, they'd grown accustomed to spending long periods in silence, not even waiting for customers, sometimes listening to music or calmly smoking joints. People came in, drifted through the narrow aisles, nosed around the objects and sometimes even bought something. Bill rang up the sales without comment, and the regulars didn't say the place had changed, or lost its spark. They sensed a displacement of energy—something that happens all the time in this part of the world without anyone getting disoriented or discombobulated, for here, in this umbilical city, all is displacement and transfiguration and change. Change and over.

Roberta has no desire to stir from the back room, which Bill has put in order or rather, cleared for her. She feels at home there, with just a big brass bed with old-fashioned cushions, a table, a chair, an easel. Austere, soothing decor. Only one element disrupts the serenity: Agustín's manuscripts in a tidy pile on the table, alongside the teapot and the damp ring left by the cup she's now holding in her hand. She doesn't want to go near the blessed manuscripts, doesn't even want to see them. Though she once thought those pages contained an answer, now she is certain she is not looking for any answer at all.

Feline at this stage, she rises in a catlike motion and goes to Bill's counter to select the most beautiful wrapping paper. She digs out a black and silver folded sheet, recycled from someone else's present, and also a green bow. Then returns without a word to the back room. Deftly and meticulously she wraps up the manuscripts.

Out of sight, out of mind, as the wry saying goes. The proper moment to transfer the goods is imminent—to present them, that is, to their legitimate owner.

For now it is enough to float in the ambiguity of worthy questions that have no concrete answer.

What could be the word written with the borrowed pen? it seems the master asked as he was dying.

Now there's an inquiry worth pursuing. Stretched out on the high bed, Roberta lets herself meander along that path. What is the word? Which leads her to ask, as well: What is the sound of one hand clapping?

And clapping for what, at this stage of the game?

From her semireclining position, Roberta looks through the window, past the easel and her own portrait with its back to her. Bill, every now and then, appears in the room, which has gradually taken on a home-sweet-home atmosphere. He has even hung a small painting.

Bill goes in and out cautiously, as if Roberta were asleep. From time to time he brings something rescued from the shop: a standing lamp, a beautiful tureen, window curtains. Roberta sometimes smiles when he picks up the pencil and works on her portrait, never when he enters with another well-chosen object. Roberta is not smiling out of happiness. She is composing her image as if to merge with her portrait and blot out memories.

The curtains don't prevent her from seeing or guessing about the passersby in the street, bulkily clad, round as bundles. Waves of disconnected thoughts besiege her and she does nothing to lure them or drive them away. Her favorite bum shows up in her memory, the one who crops up with the first buds, ever more deteriorated but alive. What hidden tunnel does he sneak into in winter? Last summer she saw him with a fur coat over his shoulders: he couldn't take it off or it might be stolen. Does he still have it?

More questions swirling around with no possibility of answers.

Or with indirect answers that emerge by unsuspected routes.

Bill in one of his sweeping flights into the back room places a large shawl over her shoulders.

"I hope you like it, it's a genuine paisley. A customer dug it out of the chaos but I refused to sell it to her, thought it was perfect for you."

Roberta the mannequin. She feels a need to be sheltered, perpetually motionless, and recognizes the anxiety for movement implicit in this need. Or the reverse. The urge to stay—there, forever—not out of sheer, primordial need but in reaction to her true urge to run off. Once again. To escape the trap.

Bill enters again and tells her, I'm closing early today—it'll be nice and quiet for us. I want to finish your portrait, I want to sketch you, every contour of you, your characters, your dreams. I want to know you. Please sit down on the chair. Lying down the way you are, I can't really see your neck, it changes the shape of your face—you look like a cat. Please sit down and look alert again.

"Today, Baby, there's a change of form. I can't move. There are days or parts of days that seem terminal. Today I've reached the end, can't move a finger—I who like dancing more than anything else, like sketching in the air with my hands. Or writing with my body. Have I told you I believed in that? I never knew how to express it clearly, but I think or used to think that I wrote with my body, with all of my being. Now I don't write with my body or with anything else."

"It may be depression. Shake it off."

"Once I was the main character in a story entitled 'Hunting

for Shells, She Came Upon a Prick.' Stories written with the body always have a title—not like my novels, which I never know how to title and when I do find one, it turns out it's already been used."

She falls silent, disinclined to tell that minimal story which was like a brushstroke of India ink on dampened paper, a sketch with blurred edges. Always looking for shells she was, at beaches, always pausing at what was tiny against the devouring vastness of the sea. She was walking among the rocks, and there were delicate shells in between the rocks, and she went along gathering them. On a rock farther on she spied the man, the man and his zipless circumstance, but couldn't turn around and escape a potentially bad moment. All she could do was keep going, pretending not to have noticed anything, continuing to gather ever more spectacular shells, Gretel following a trail of crumbs toward the fatal gingerbread prick.

Well. Basically nothing serious ever happens (ever?).

Bill, a bit anxious at her silence, questions her, finally is given a rundown of the situation, and insists on knowing the end of the story and whether it was a story.

"Nothing happened. I don't know, I paid no attention finally. Never found out whether he was a flasher or a satyr or someone who had a weak bladder or something of the sort. I simply wanted to tell you how at certain moments I feel that I'm writing with the body, going along as though tracing out words, giving it a title, and then incarnating the metonymy, the physical displacement."

Ever driven by a possibly suicidal impulse, poking around in the middle of the night into the most sordid nooks, looking for something more. Perhaps a way out.

"Let me join you then. With your beautiful body we could write a certain porno story I've had in mind. A collaboration."

"Nobody wants to risk a novel."

"Are you taking that risk?"

"Me neither, not a novel—with you, I mean."

"A porno story is something else."

"But not now, no. Give me a small advance for now, a kiss—the rest we'll leave for later. I promise. Now if I make a move, it'll have to be a move out of here, to run an errand. There's still some cargo to deliver."

"You're repeating yourself, Rob. Unworthy of you. Are you about to go running off again in the middle of the night?"

"It's only seven o'clock. I'll meet you, if you want, at my place at nine. I've got to go home and recuperate a little. If I stay here, I'll just crash on these cushions forever."

"Forever? You're too mercurial, ever on the move. I don't think there's any danger of that."

It was shortly after midnight and they had just awakened, when the downstairs buzzer roused them from their drowsiness. Hector came out of his bedroom to answer, concealing his apprehension, thought Agustín, who could conceal nothing.

"Lara's here," Hector told him, and soon Lara herself arrived brimming with news.

"You missed dear Edouard's funeral. It was terribly moving and ecumenical, even though the gravediggers absolutely refused to work on Christmas Day. Christmas is a day of birth and not of death, they said, and Antoine had to butter them up and use all his powers of persuasion, which are considerable. He told them the story of Ed's life and about the Ballets Russes, he told them about ancient traditions, completely invented, of course, and he told them that in Russia—in the times of the czars, naturally, not of the disgusting Communists, as they say, a burial on Christmas Day was a good omen. Due to the life cycle, the winter solstice, things of that sort and others that the boys tacked on because, thank God, they're not short on imagination. Lucky for all who were present, especially the gravediggers, turning up Mother Earth to sow the beneficient fertilizer which will eventually sprout, as you know, and the fertilizer of art to cap it off, as you can imagine, knowing the boys. In addition they brought along bottles of champagne but not a single flower, they wanted absolutely no flowers at the funeral, only mistletoe wreaths, to preserve the spirit of the occasion, and glass balls, assorted Christmas decorations, evergreen branches. You can't beat the boys when it comes to pageantry. There were even balalaikas.

Several old men who sit at the northeast corner of Washington Square in the summertime pining for the steppes and spend their winter in mothballs, I suppose—the boys took them out of mothballs and brought them to the foot of Ed's grave. They played with such feeling. There were hordes of people, all the dancers of the New York City Ballet, and loads of Ed's other disciples getting on in years. They would've liked to dance but couldn't because of the cold, and bulky coats, and also because not everyone has Mark and Antoine's sense of fantasy—and here, they've sent you a bottle of Veuve Clicquot, don't know the year, that Ed put aside for Hector for this very special occasion, they said, and have also sent him Ed's jewel box at the express wish of the deceased. They asked that you take special care of the tinsel rings they themselves made for him, they were the old man's favorites. The boys told me to tell you all that—and they've permanently closed off the passageway, forcing me to face the elements. I also have something for Agustín the mumbler. Roberta didn't go to the funeral but she came to see me at around eight—I'm receiving condolences, like a member of the family. She asked nonchalantly for Agustín and I told her that I thought the two of you might have gone over to the House of Puppets. It occurred to me because you'd asked me to loan you Frieda. Then Roberta, bursting with Christmas spirit, gave me this beautiful and rather heavy package with a green bow to deliver to Agustín with all her best wishes, and said for him to enjoy it. And having fulfilled my noble Michael Strogoff or beef Stroganoff mission or whatever it is, I herewith retire but not without reclaiming first my priceless Frieda who I hope hasn't been subjected to unspeakable indignities, if I make myself clear."

She flung her scarf over her shoulder as if it were a feathered boa, picked up her huge deflated handbag, and headed for the door. Agustín cut her off in the hall.

"Where's Roberta? I keep calling and she doesn't answer, or have her answering machine on."

"Keep trying, keep trying. I have a hunch she'll be back home one of these days."

*O*ne is struck by the perfect tempo of this story, which unfolds with the precision of a musical composition. Defying the categorization of genres, it has been put forward as a pornographic work, owing perhaps to the sheer nakedness of its protagonists, but the subtle eroticism and romanticism throughout belie that notion. The linguistic play of the coauthors—also protagonists of the work—is noteworthy, as is the constant stylistic tension, which fosters various levels of reading and threatens to reach an untimely culmination. The climax, however, is cleverly controlled, achieving heights of unsuspected dialectic intensity, which, though cast in a purely classical mold, archaic even, incorporates surprising postmodernist modulations.

An analysis of the foci of canonization and cleavage, clashes and inflections within the discipline enables us to discern a counterpoint of passions that opposes, contradicts, contrasts, and finally integrates the semantic values.

In this text where reading/writing unfolds in synchronicity, the exploratory dimension of the phallogocentric signifier is of particular note, skewing above and below the ambiguous signified of matriarchal matrix.

The tongue (language) is taken deeply to heart, with free usage of onomatopoeia and pleonasm, without shying away from a liberal measure of crude, vernacular expressions. The keen sensitivity of the coauthors eschews verbiage and resists becoming enmeshed in grammatical and/or lexicographic intricacies, yet is *mindful occasionally of the bilingualism functioning as shifter in this hyperactive text.*

We are dealing with a story at once transparent and obscure, pervaded, we would say, with the problematic of our times. Its scope is striking, most unusual in light of the genre to which it properly belongs; its perfectly calibrated alliterations and iterations delight us, distract from the apparent improvisation, and suggest an elaborate, austere rewriting.

The frequent instances of off-color passages are provocative and aesthetically valid, the gears of the various tropes meshing smoothly, lubricated to the maximum, without allowing the inevitable and even desirable rhythmical and metrical irregularities to obstruct the natural unfolding of the plot.

At this point the ongoing crescendo becomes paroxysmic and the lyricism of the opening gives way to a seamless creative intensity.

The final gasp is not surprising, but within the framework of this cursory criticism one can only designate it as a literary happy ending, a truly seminal, semantic achievement.

"Our porno story turned out well, even though the bodies were kind of exhausted."

"Very well. A pity that these writings with the body don't get into print. To send to *Playboy,* I mean."

"A masterpiece of its genre."

"Right."

And they fell sound asleep.

Roberta is attending a very crowded party, chatting, moving about, wandering among people she doesn't know or thinks she doesn't know or doesn't recognize. Suddenly, out of nowhere, she feels an impact in the middle of her forehead, like an admonition. She begins to fall slowly, very slowly, and then she is lying on a high bed or a table and beside her are two shadows. Two men. She must tell one of them that she loves him, always did love him and could never express it. The moment has come, but when she opens her mouth, not words but a sudden gush of blood comes out. She knows they have shot her, that she's going to die, and the worst of it is that she must leave without having said what can now never be said. With tremendous effort she extends her hand toward the chosen shadow in the hope that the man will understand her message, when

a sound, far far away,

begins to bring her

back to these shores.

Awakening came in waves, and some of the waves turned her over, drawing her again into the world of shadows. The sound persisted. Roberta could see herself in her bed, between her own sheets. Still in her dream, she slowly stretched out her hand in a wide sweep. Who would the chosen one be, that shadow—

The phone was ringing.

The aroma of coffee and toast returned her to disconcerting, domestic reality, and indicated Bill's location.

"You answer," she shouted, unable to stir from the bed.

Bill picked up the receiver in the kitchen and immediately stuck his head out to say, It's Agustín—take it on the other phone.

No, no, Roberta signaled, wagging her index finger. No.

Bill ducked back into the kitchen to carry out her simple request, and Roberta began talking to the empty room.

"Tell him I found the word. The one that's written with a borrowed pen. Big discovery, tell him, it's the same little old four-letter word. All so elementary, so impossible. So easy and so hard and so hackneyed. Tell him the word is—no, don't tell him anything. He has to find it on his own, tell him."

Bill emerged from the kitchen with the breakfast tray.

"Don't waste your breath, kiddo. He already hung up. Said he just called to thank you, insisted I tell you that finally he's going to be able to bury his dead."

"The dead you kill . . ." Roberta began, and burst out laughing.

Bill looked at her blankly, unable from his side of the language barrier to fill in the rest of the classic line: ". . . are in good health."

Roberta in any case offered him a version more in keeping with the circumstances.

"The dead you kill are offspring of someone else's crimes."

"You Argentine novelists—"